## "Run?" Val echoed incredulously. "Why would you tell me to—?"

This was no time for debate. Instead of biting off a few choice words of explanation, Rafe grabbed her hand. Rather than pushing her ahead of him, he went the other route. He pulled her in his wake.

Hard.

And then she finally heard it. She heard the cause for his alarm. The sound of something pounding on the ground seemed as if it was reverberating right through her, like an earthquake in the distance.

The "earthquake" felt as though it was coming closer by the moment.

Val turned her head in the direction the sound was coming from.

That was when she saw it.

A bull.

A huge black bull was charging directly at them.

Dear Reader,

Forever, Texas started out as a onetime, one-book idea. One story, about a sheriff and an abandoned baby—and the lady lawyer looking not just for the baby but her runaway sister, as well. But once she—and I—"came" to Forever, the people I wrote about tended to stick in my mind. The main two characters got to play out their story, but what about the others? What about the sheriff's deputy, Alma, and her five brothers? What about his sister, Ramona? And then there was the heroine's sister, not to mention Miss Joan, the lady with the slightly too-red hair who ran the diner and oversaw everyone else's lives. What about all their stories? So I decided to start exploring those avenues, finding out what made these people tick. What made them happy.

This time around, we come to Gabe's twin brother, Rafe, a rancher content with his lot and pretty much minding his own business—until he stumbles across a vivacious woman with a camera, taking pictures of his land. She turns out to be a location scout for a film company—and wouldn't you just know it, she thinks that his family's ranch and the town of Forever are a perfect place to shoot their new movie.

By the end of the story, the term *perfect location* takes on a whole new meaning for Valentine Jones and for Rafe. And Miguel Rodriguez now has just two sons left to marry off. Who will it be next? Curious? Y'all come back now, y'hear?

In conclusion, as always, I thank you for reading. I wouldn't be here without you. And from the bottom of my heart I wish you someone to love who loves you back.

All the best,

Marie

# HIS FOREVER VALENTINE

—

## MARIE FERRARELLA

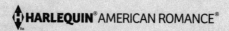

Recycling programs
for this product may
not exist in your area.

ISBN-13: 978-0-373-75466-3

HIS FOREVER VALENTINE

Copyright © 2013 by Marie Rydzynski-Ferrarella

**Printed in U.S.A.**

# ABOUT THE AUTHOR

Marie Ferrarella, a *USA TODAY* bestselling and RITA® Award—winning author, has written more than two hundred books for Harlequin, some under the name Marie Nicole. Her romances are beloved by fans worldwide. Visit her website, www.marieferrarella.com.

## Books by Marie Ferrarella

To
Anastasia Ault
Who Makes Me Remember
Why I Write

# Chapter One

She was gorgeous.

Had he forgotten his tan Stetson at the house, the way he occasionally did, Raphael Rodriguez might have been inclined to believe that he'd gotten sunstroke and was having his very first hallucination.

But his Stetson was firmly planted on his head—he actually reached up to touch the brim to make sure it was there. And, although it was rather warm for the middle of January—winters here in Forever, Texas, *were* usually mild—it's wasn't *that* hot. At least, not hot enough to produce either heatstroke or mirages. This morning, initially, there'd even been a slight nip in the air to remind him that winter wasn't quite finished with them yet.

All in all, this had been a more eventful winter than usual, at least for his family. It had been a winter where his twin brother, Gabriel, had found the girl of his dreams. Gabe and the woman he called "Angel" were getting married in April.

Rafe had to admit—although only silently to himself—that he was somewhat envious of his twin.

Angel was incredibly sweet and he'd never seen Gabe so happy. At times, the man seemed to be walking five inches off the ground.

The thought of finding someone of his own to settle down with had been on Rafe's mind a great deal lately.

Was that why he thought he saw this gorgeous vision in the distance now? She couldn't be real. Not this beautiful redhead with a killer body standing smack dab in the middle of his ranch.

His *family's* ranch, Rafe amended. The property belonged to his family in the truest sense of the word since their father, Miguel Sr., had changed the deed to the ranch from listing him as the sole owner to putting down all their names, dividing the property in equal shares between all of them.

That particular action had come about at their father's insistence because they'd all had a part in keeping the bank from foreclosing on the ranch. Each one of them had gotten at least a part-time job, turning over their meager paychecks to their father so that he could stay abreast of the mortgage *and* their late mother's mountain of medical bills. That selfless act, the senior Rodriguez had said, was what entitled them to an equal share of the sprawling ranch.

As he drove his Jeep in closer, Rafe couldn't take his eyes off her.

A woman like that looked completely out of place in a place like this. She *had* to be a figment of his imagination. But he'd already figured out that he wasn't experiencing sunstroke and all he'd had to eat this morning were scrambled eggs and some coffee that could have been labeled as solid. The regular housekeeper was on vacation visiting her sister so it had been Miguel Jr.'s turn to cook, or do whatever it was that his oldest brother *felt* passed for cooking.

But Mike kept things simple, so it was safe to say that Rafe hadn't ingested anything that would have caused a hallucination like this in the middle of his morning.

Steadily decreasing the distance between them, Rafe couldn't help wondering when the woman was going to disappear. He couldn't get over the feeling that she just might be a mirage created by his brain because he was currently without female companionship and Eli, Alma and Gabe were all either married or spoken for.

Was *that* why he was having this vision?

He'd driven out here to the northern region of the ranch for a reason. He was looking over the miles of fencing, searching for a hole or a break in it anywhere. At last count, they were short a few head of cattle. Since it was doubtful that anyone in the area would actually bother to rustle a meager five or six head, his father thought that the cattle might have just wandered off because of a break in the fencing, most likely caused by the spate of inclement weather they'd just experienced.

"Either that, or the coyotes around here have learned how to steal and use wire cutters," Ramon—who preferred being called Ray—had cracked at the table this morning before breakfast.

Rafe had been quick to volunteer to be the one to drive the length of the fence, checking for a break. If he hadn't he would have been stuck with kitchen cleanup. Given the choice, he would always rather be outdoors, even driving around for hours, than stuck washing and drying dishes. It wasn't that he viewed that kind of work as "woman's work," just "indoor" work. Time out in the open won out every time.

But this vision was inexplicable. And she wasn't vanishing.

The woman, with her needle-straight hair—hair the color of the sun's first blush at sunrise—dipping halfway down her slender back, was still there.

Anticipation telegraphed through Rafe's body, putting his pulse on high alert.

Now that he was getting close enough to discern details more clearly, Rafe saw that she was doing something other than taking in the view. She was preoccupied taking pictures with a camera that appeared way too large and sturdy for a typical tourist. She wasn't just some outsider who'd lost her way and had decided to pause and take a few pictures of the land she'd wandered onto.

She looked to him to be a woman with a mission.

Part of him would have opted to stop driving and just watch her for a little while. Watch her moving about, looking as close to poetic as the photographs she appeared to be framing.

But just as he was considering shutting off his car engine and silently observing her, the slender woman with the flowing strawberry-red hair turned around to look at him.

She was even more striking from the front than she was from the back.

And she was looking straight at him.

Her smile was infectious. Rather than sound generic, the one-word greeting she offered him somehow seemed incredibly personal. "Hi."

"Hi," Rafe echoed. For a moment, he just sat there in his Jeep, looking at her. Unable to make a move.

Maybe she *was* a hallucination after all. The woman seemed completely unfazed at being discovered trespassing. There was no uneasiness or discomfort over the fact that he'd discovered her in a place she clearly didn't belong.

In his experience, the few tourists that drifted through Forever eyed the local population a bit warily, as if they weren't quite sure just how civilized these "natives" actually were—if they ate with utensils or still used their fingers when they were consuming their meals.

The thought had the corners of his mouth curving.

The woman, he noted, also, wasn't making any breathless confessions as to why she was trespassing, nor was she launching into any kind of an elaborate explanation as to what she was doing here this far from town.

As a matter of fact, she wasn't saying anything at all, which struck Rafe as rather unique. In his experience, women usually took charge of the conversation and, on the average, did a hell of a lot more talking than men.

At least his sister Alma made it seem that way.

Rafe turned off his vehicle's engine as an afterthought and got out of the Jeep.

The woman had lowered her camera and was now watching him much the way he had been watching her.

Except that she had what he could only call a bemused expression on her face.

Was there some joke he was missing, or was that just her way of trying to disarm him?

Whatever it was, it was working.

He started the conversation with the obvious by asking her, "You do know that you're on private land, right?"

Her smile answered him before her words did. It was as if there was some silent communication going on.

Definitely a hallucination, he couldn't help thinking one final time.

"Yes, I do," she replied, still wearing that wide, inviting grin, "and I think that this is exactly what my boss is look for."

So she was a real estate agent? It hardly seemed likely. He'd never seen her before and Forever was not exactly destined to become a thriving metropolis in the next decade or so. Everyone in town had at least a nodding acquaintance with everyone else who lived in or around the area—unless they were strangers, fresh from some other place.

Since he didn't want the woman wasting her time and his, there was only one answer he could give her. "It's not for sale."

There was no way that anyone in his family would be willing to part with the ranch, or even the smallest section of the ranch. This land was far more than just square footage to them. It was their heritage, it was tied to their childhood and more importantly, it was their invisible connection with their mother. You didn't sell something like that no matter what the offer turned out to be.

"Oh, he wouldn't want to buy it," the sexy woman informed him brightly. "If I'm right about this—and I usually am," she added without the slightest bit of bravado or vanity, "he'll be interested in renting it."

Rafe's deep brown eyes narrowed beneath his tan Stetson. He tried desperately to make sense out of what the redhead was telling him. He guessed that brains didn't come along with the beauty. Such a shame.

"Renting it?" he questioned. That really wasn't an option, either. "I'm sorry, but—"

Rafe didn't get a chance to turn her down. Lowering her camera so that it now just hung from a strap, its lens pointing, unfocused, at the ground, she moved closer to him.

"Wait," she requested, raising her voice just enough to register a tad louder than his. "Hear me out, please." She gestured around the terrain with open enthusiasm. "This place is absolutely perfect."

"And we intend to keep it that way," he told her in no uncertain terms.

Gorgeous or not, he wasn't about to let himself be turned around by the woman and make promises he had no right to make nor keep, even if he could—which he couldn't. Everything that went on at the ranch was decided by a vote—and they all had a vote. So he couldn't accept any offers she might make.

It really didn't matter what the knockout in the sexy jeans that adhered to her like a second skin had in mind or was going to say.

He supposed that, in all fairness, he should hear her out. Let the woman talk. And then he would give her the bottom line: the Rodriguez land was not for sale.

"I guess maybe leasing it would be a better term for what I'm proposing." She turned to face him directly. Her eyes were dancing and he found them absolutely mesmerizing—not that this changed the situation. "In my opinion, this place is absolutely perfect."

Well, that certainly echoed his feelings on the subject. He had never experienced an iota of wanderlust. Forever was where he belonged. Specifically, on the family ranch.

"We like to think so," he responded. "But this has also been in the family for several generations now and we don't—"

Again, the woman interrupted him before he could finish his sentence and terminate the conversation. "We'd put it back just the way we found it," she promised. "We've got a great cleanup crew."

He stopped the protest that was on his lips and looked at her. Just who was "we?" And he had another question.

"Cleanup crew?" he asked. "You travel with a cleanup crew?" Who included that in their entourage? Just what did this woman do for a living?

"I don't," she clarified, "but the production company does." And then she laughed, realizing that, as usual, she'd gotten ahead of herself. "Maybe I should start at the beginning."

"Maybe you should," he agreed, waiting for her to start making some sense.

Reaching into the pocket of the fringed vest she was

wearing, the woman plucked out a business card and offered it to him. At the same time, she told him what was written on it.

"I'm Valentine Jones—Val to my friends," she interjected. She didn't expect the name to mean anything to him, although within the business, she was beginning to build up a fairly good reputation. "And I'm a location scout."

Rafe glanced down at the card she'd handed him. There was a colorful logo on it that looked vaguely familiar, but he couldn't place it. He only knew he'd seen it before, but on a larger scale. He offered to give her back her card, but she shook her head, silently indicating that he should keep it for future reference.

Not that there would be any, he thought, resigned.

"At the risk of sounding ignorant, what's a location scout?" he asked.

Rather than laugh at the question, the way he half expected her to, Val flashed a smile at him that was equal parts understanding and unsettlingly sensual.

"I'm surprised you haven't been approached about this before now. A location scout is exactly what it sounds like—I scout different locations."

He saw no reason for that. "Why?"

"For movies," she answered simply.

Her mother had been a starlet with a minor degree of success and fame. She had moved on to be a far more successful casting director, while her father was a well-known and much-in-demand cinematographer. Movies and Hollywood had *always* been part of her life. At times, it was hard for her to remember that a good many people she dealt with were outside the industry and as such, had to be educated as to what she did.

Rafe was trying to make sense out of what she was telling him. "You mean like for a movie theater? You're looking to build a movie theater out here?" he asked incredulously. This definitely was off the beaten path. It would make far more sense to put up more movie theaters in the center of town, next to the one they already had.

"No, I'm looking to *film* a movie here." That made it sound as if she was the one who made the movie and she wasn't. "Or rather, my boss is—or he will be once I send him these pictures I just took." Again, Val realized she was getting ahead of herself. There were questions she had to ask first. "The ranch house I saw coming out here was absolutely perfect for the story, just the right blend of old-fashioned and modern. You *are* the owner, right?" she looked at him hopefully.

Rafe inclined his head. "I'm one of them."

Val experienced what she could only term was a slight sinking, disappointed feeling gelling in the pit of her stomach. "Your wife?" she asked, guessing as to who the other owner was.

Rafe laughed as he shook his head. "More like my father and my siblings," he clarified.

"Siblings," Val echoed, nodding her head. The sinking feeling disappeared as if it hadn't been there to begin with. She could feel her mouth curving. "Siblings are good," she pronounced.

"They seem to think so," Rafe told her. "And that goes for my father, too," he added.

Val nodded. She'd heard him specify his father the first time. It looked like she was about to present her case before a committee. Nothing she hadn't done before. She'd been with Sinclair Productions for a few years now and during that time, she'd encountered a whole range of home owners from a single, hermit-like owner to a holding company she had to spend days tracking down. She'd pleaded her boss's case before all of them.

"I'd like to meet these siblings and your dad so I could talk to them and see if there's anything I can do or say to convince them to give their permission to use this ranch as a backdrop of the film we're making. No sense in my sending on these photos to the director if it's just to tease him and raise his hopes, only to find out that your siblings and dad won't let us film here."

The way she phrased it, he got the feeling that she had just arbitrarily had him throwing in his lot with her. Although he now saw no harm in it, he didn't want her just taking it for granted, either. He wanted to hear the woman's pitch first—just in case there was something she hadn't mentioned or that he was overlooking.

"I didn't say I'd be all right with it," he reminded her.

He didn't have to. She could feel the way he was leaning. But, for the sake of his pride, she played along.

The woman named Val turned her face up to his and it occurred to Rafe that he had never looked into such a soulful pair of eyes before.

"And there's nothing I can say to get you to throw your lot in with us? We pay well. I've looked at a great many different places and this is the first one that struck me as being perfect. It's so unspoiled and pristine—"

He could all but channel what his father and siblings would say. Money had never been their prime motivation and even less now, since they were no longer strapped.

"And we'd like to keep it that way," he told her. That was what was important, keeping the land productive and beautiful.

"I completely understand and we can write that into the contract. That if we don't leave this place exactly as pristine as we found it, then the fees for using it while filming our movie will be doubled." Val detected some resistance in his face. "I might be able to get my boss to triple it."

Given what she was saying, Rafe could only come to one conclusion. "Then he *will* leave it in bad shape."

"No," she said firmly, "he'll be triply inspired to make sure no one leaves behind so much as a candy wrapper tumbling about in the wind."

She moved just a shade closer to him. "What do you say?"

If ever someone had deserved to hear the word yes—

Rafe's eyes widened as the thought suddenly froze in his mind.

Observing him, for a second, Val was certain that she had him. But then he grabbed her by the shoulders, pushing her to move ahead of him. "I say, *run!*"

## Chapter Two

Stunned, Val held her ground. His response made no sense to her. What did it have to do with what she'd just asked him?

"What?" she demanded.

"Run!" Rafe repeated, this time shouting the word at her.

Was this some sort of a joke? Val stared at the cowboy in confusion. She still didn't understand why he'd say something like that.

"Run?" Val echoed incredulously. "Why would you tell me to…?"

This was no time for a debate. Instead of biting off a few choice words of explanation, Rafe grabbed her hand. Rather than pushing her ahead of him, he went the other route. He pulled her in his wake.

Hard.

And then she finally heard it. She heard the cause for his alarm. The sound of something pounding on the ground felt as if it reverberated right through her, like an earthquake in the distance.

The "earthquake" felt like it was coming closer by the moment.

Val turned her head in the direction the sound was coming from.

That was when she saw it.

A bull.

A huge, black bull was charging directly at them.

At her.

Val needed no further incentive to take flight. A veteran of several marathons—every one of them undertaken for some sort of a good cause—she immediately upped her game. With her pouring it on, Rafe no longer had to pull her in his wake. Despite the situation, a hint of admiration at her speed filled him when he realized that she was now keeping up with him and that at any moment she was going to pull ahead of him.

"He's gaining on us!" Val cried, beginning to realize that just maybe this competition between the charging bull and them might not end well after all.

Less than a minute later, Val saw that they were not just running *from* something, they were running *toward* something. Directly up ahead was a long stretch of wire fencing.

"Will that keep him from trampling us?" she managed to ask as she continued running alongside of Rafe for all she was worth.

"It damn well better," was all he allowed himself to say.

There was no point in telling her that he had a plan B. That if worse had come to worst and Valentine had frozen with fear, he'd been prepared to divert the beast, to get the bull's attention so that it would run after him rather than attack the woman who had turned up on his property unannounced like this. Rafe hadn't been raised to subscribe to the "every man for himself" school of thought. His father would have never allowed it.

But luckily, the woman with the improbable first name was not only sexy as hell, she was fit, which in this case meant that she was capable of keeping up with him and—for now—keeping ahead of Jasper, the whimsical name that Alma had awarded the bull that they had bought a year ago to breed with some of their cattle.

Reaching the fence less than a minute ahead of the charging bull, Rafe quickly pushed his uninvited guest up and over the fence. The next second, he dove over it himself. Rafe managed to clear it—all except for his left boot, the tip of which got caught on the very edge of the fence.

What began as a clean execution became less so as he found himself falling short of his intended mark.

Rather than hitting the grass, Rafe landed on top of Val, who was just in the process of turning around. Instead of gaining her feet, she gained added weight. Enough weight to push the air right out of her.

A startled cry, comprised of protest and surprise, echoed through the morning air, riding on the air he had knocked out of her.

As for him, Rafe was acutely aware that what he was on top of bore no resemblance to either the ground or the grass. It was soft, warm, enticingly fragrant and damn stirring. His body absorbed the sensations before his mind could even frame them.

Banking down the major part of his reaction, he allowed his concern to come to the foreground. Though he'd attempted to buffer his weight, he *had* come down rather hard on her.

"Are you all right?" he asked.

Right now she couldn't help thinking she was really far from all right, but not in the sense he meant it. Generally warm and outgoing, Val still kept a part of herself in reserve. The part that had, at the age of nineteen, run off with Scott Walters, a ruggedly handsome stuntman with the gift of always saying the right thing. He'd been her first love and she had loved him fiercely. Until, recklessly, he'd unintentionally broken her heart.

Since that day, she had carefully guarded her heart and kept a tight rein on her emotions. That went hand in hand with not trusting any physical reaction she might have to a good-looking man. Even a good-looking man who was trying to save her from being gored.

"I don't think anything's broken." She saw him nod with relief, but other than that, he seemed to be making no attempt to get up. Was the man posing for a still life? "You can get off me now," Val prompted.

The moment the words were out of her mouth, Rafe realized that he was not just partially on top of her, he was *completely* on top of her, the way a bodyguard might be with the person he was trying to protect at the very first sound of gunfire.

The imprint of her body was telegraphing itself to his torso in big, bold, capital letters. It took him a second to come to.

"Oh, yeah, right." Rafe paused for half a beat to look

over his shoulder and make sure that the bull had come to a stop and was still on his side of the fence.

Jasper was indeed there, and whatever pending rage had sent the animal charging right for them had clearly disappeared. The bull had stopped charging, stopped running and instead of pawing the ground as expected, the bull was now docilely examining what appeared to be a dandelion nestled in the midst of a light green carpet comprised of new shoots of grass.

Belatedly, Rafe replayed the woman's words in his head and this time, he scrambled up to his feet, separating their two bodies despite the vast appeal of remaining pressed together for the duration of the morning.

Once up, he offered his hand to her.

Val looked at it for a moment, as if she was debating ignoring it and just bouncing up of her own accord. But this was no time to establish boundaries and if he wanted to help her up, she knew she should just accept it without making a fuss.

Val wrapped her fingers around the offered hand, trying not to dwell on the fact that her body was still tingling. It made her acutely aware of the fact that their two bodies had mingled as much as was physically possible, given the fact that their clothes had remained on and they weren't engaging in any sort of a romantic liaison.

The moment she was up on her feet, Val quickly dusted herself off. She watched the bull warily out of the corner of her eye. As incredible as it seemed, the animal appeared to be almost subdued. Given his previous behavior, how was that even possible?

"You train him to do that?" she finally asked her so-called rescuer.

Rafe had no idea what she was talking about. "Excuse me?"

Val jerked a thumb in the bull's direction. "Did you train him to come charging up out of nowhere like that?" she asked.

If he *had* trained the bull, there might be a position for this man on the set, she thought. They could never have too many animal trainers on board when they were filming this kind of movie.

Rafe looked at her uncertainly. He'd heard about Hollywood types, about how they lived in a world of their own making, but this was his first encounter with someone from that city and he was the type who always wanted to make sense of things, to understand them.

That caused him to ask, "Why would I do something like that?"

Val continued to brush bits and pieces of dirt and grass from her clothing and hair. "I would think that might be self-explanatory," she told him, looking at Rafe pointedly.

Maybe she meant nothing by it. At any event, he supposed he should count himself lucky that she wasn't screaming at him, or having a tantrum. So he laughed, shaking his head.

"I'm not an animal whisperer, if that's what you're getting at," he assured her. "Jasper is his own bull and does whatever he wants to. My father bought him not that long ago for breeding purposes. So far, he's shown more of an interest in playing poker than in mating with any of the candidates we've paraded in front of him. To tell the truth, this is the most alive I've seen Jasper since his former owner dropped him off."

The bull, from what she could see, was now wandering off again. Feeling a little safer, her heart stopped beating wildly.

"Maybe he'd behave a little more macho if you changed his name to Bruce," she suggested, watching the animal retreat.

Rafe grinned at the proposal. He sincerely doubted that the bull understood English. "A bull by any other name…" His voice trailed off as his grin grew in size.

She cocked an eyebrow at the attempted quotation. "Shakespeare?"

"Paraphrased," Rafe allowed good-naturedly. "Anyway, I don't think his name has very much—if anything—to do with his behavior." The grin faded slightly as he became serious. "You sure you didn't hurt anything?" His eyes swept over her.

She could almost feel them passing right over her body. This man, she had a feeling, would have fit right in with the men back in Hollywood. Something about him stirred the imagination—as well as her blood.

"Just my pride," she answered.

His brow furrowed slightly. Pausing, Rafe bent down to pick up his Stetson and dusted it off. "I don't think I understand. What does your pride have to do with anything?"

"I'm not exactly accustomed to being tossed over a fence and landing on my butt," she replied, nodding at the fence.

From where he stood, there was nothing to be embarrassed about. Survival came first. "My guess is that you're probably not accustomed to running from a charging bull, either."

She laughed. "Can't say I am," Val admitted.

The woman was being an awfully good sport about this, Rafe thought, feeling magnanimous toward her. "You want to come up to the house?"

"To talk to your father?" she asked a little uncertainly.

Having grown up in the world that she had, acting and masking her thoughts were second nature to her. Otherwise, her uneasiness at the invitation might have been evident. She did want to meet with whoever it was that could give her permission to use this property for the film, but how did she know for certain that there'd be anyone there? The prospect of being alone with a man she found more than a little attractive made her feel somewhat nervous.

Val didn't consider herself a timid woman by any means, but she wasn't a foolish one, either, and in her book, that meant not taking any undue chances or going off to meetings on her own with complete strangers. Even good-looking ones.

*Especially* good-looking ones, she amended.

"That was what you wanted, wasn't it?" Rafe asked her. Then, before she could answer, he added, "I feel as if I owe you, seeing as how you weren't expecting to go for an impromptu run when you came out here. For a Hollywood girl, you can certainly run."

The comment made her wonder what sort of stereotypical image he had of Hollywood women. "I didn't want to wind up on his trophy wall," she told him, nodding in the direction that the bull had taken.

"I wouldn't have let that happen." He wasn't bragging; he just wanted her to be reassured that while she was here, she was safe.

Her eyes swept over him as if she was looking for something. "What were you planning on doing, whipping out your bullfighting cape and distract him away from me?" she asked.

There was laughter in her eyes, Rafe noticed. She probably thought he was trying to make himself appear important after the fact—not that he could really fault her for that.

"No, but I would have run in another direction, after distracting Jasper and getting him to follow me."

The humor slowly faded from her eyes, replaced by a look of fascination. "You're actually serious," she realized.

"Why wouldn't I be?" Rafe asked. "We don't get too many people passing through Forever, and getting one of them trampled by a bull wouldn't exactly look very friendly on the tourist website," he answered tongue-in-cheek.

The humor returned to her bright blue eyes. "I guess it wouldn't at that." She glanced back at the bull, who had apparently lost interest in both of them and was now ambling back to wherever he had initially come from. "Is he just trying to lure us into a trap by giving us a false sense of security?"

Rafe laughed. "You're giving Jasper *way* too much

credit. He doesn't have any unusual powers of deduction. He just lost interest in us, you know, out of sight, out of mind."

She nodded knowingly at the information. "In other words, he's a typical male."

"Ouch." Rafe pretended to wince as if the words carried with them a physical blow. "What sort of men have you been encountering?"

Val deliberately blocked out any thoughts of Scott. That was way too sensitive a subject for her to discuss with a stranger. As for the other men she'd encountered, well, they were far more concerned with having a good time and moving on. For the most part, they were as shallow as puddles.

"The kind that like to sweet-talk women into things, then be on their merry way," she answered. The way she raised her chin and tossed her hair over her shoulder made Rafe feel that they were not just talking in vague generalities.

He also had the feeling that there would be no specifics forthcoming at this juncture—they didn't know each other nearly well enough for her to be capable of sharing something of importance with him.

Of course, if she stuck around, there was always that possibility that they would grow to know each other better. The idea had more than a little appeal for him.

"For the sake of argument," he began.

A never-flagging sense of curiosity had always been a shortcoming of hers—or at least she viewed it as a shortcoming. That still didn't keep her from wanting to know things. *Every*thing.

"Yes?"

Rafe tried to sound nonchalant as he asked his question, but he had a feeling that he wasn't quite successful. "If my father and the rest of us agree to having your boss film this movie on our ranch, would you be here for the duration of the filming?"

"If my boss doesn't need me to find any other locations for the film, then yes, I get to stick around." She posed a question of her own. "Why?"

Rafe shrugged just a wee bit too casually. "No reason," he answered. "Just wanted to get all my facts straight before I bring you up to the house—in case my father wants to know something after you leave."

She watched him carefully as she asked, "Then you were serious about letting me talk to your father?" Val did her best not to appear too excited, but unlike her mother, she had never been a very good poker player.

"Why wouldn't I be?"

"I don't know you yet," she said truthfully. "I thought maybe you got your kicks out of leading outsiders on."

"I don't," he assured her. The way he said it made her think he meant it. Or maybe she just wanted to believe that people in a place like this were really the salt of the earth. Uncomplicated and kind hearted. She could use that sort of thing about now.

Rafe saw her looking around uneasily. "Something the matter?"

"I'm just wondering if another bull is going to come galloping out of nowhere if I start to head toward my car."

"Nothing to worry about," he answered. "Jasper's our only bull right now. Leon passed on."

"Leon," she repeated. These people definitely did *not* give their bulls normal names. "Another nonfunctioning bull?" was her first guess.

The thought made Rafe laugh. "On the contrary, Leon functioned all too well for his own good. I think the poor guy wore himself out and spread himself a little too thin among the ladies." He grinned. "My dad said that he would rather romance the ladies than eat."

"Are we still talking about the bull?" she deadpanned. "Or have we moved on to your father?"

This time Rafe laughed heartily for a couple of minutes. When he finally stopped, he said, "I think my dad's going to like you, Valentine Jones."

If that's what it took to secure filming rights, she was ready to be downright adorable. "Well, for the sake of *Cowboys and India,* I certainly hope so."

He looked at her, a little bemused. "Cowboys and India?" he asked. What was that?

She nodded. "I guess I didn't mention it. That's the name of the movie we're making. It's about a dude ranch," she explained, adding, perhaps in hindsight unnecessarily. "It's a romantic comedy." Because he said nothing, she felt compelled to tell him, "I read the script. It's really pretty good."

"Are you required to do that?" he asked, curious.

"To read the script?" she guessed. "No, not really. But I like to so I can get a feel for the kind of setting I'm looking for. It helps me when I'm scouting out locations."

That wasn't what he was referring to. Rafe shook his head. "No, I mean are you required to say that the script is pretty good?"

Did he think she was just a puppet for the front office? Someone whose true calling was just to rubber-stamp everything? To say whatever was expedient just to get things to move along in the direction that the production department wanted it to move? She couldn't think of a more awful, colorless way to earn a living.

"Why would you think that?" she asked. "I'm not selling tickets to it."

"No, what I thought was that *you* might think that would help convince someone to give you access to their property."

She laughed. "That's not what does the convincing," she told him. "The money that the studio is willing to pay for the use of the property is supposed to do all the convincing on that level," she told him.

"Money's nice," he readily agreed. "But it's not at the top of my dad's list."

She laughed softly and to herself. "Money's at the top of everyone's list."

If his father was going to have them shoot the movie here, she'd learn otherwise, Rafe thought.

For now, he decided to say nothing.

# Chapter Three

Restless, Miguel Rodriguez was getting ready to drive out to the west end of his property to see if his son had had any luck in finding the break in the fence. It'd been a while since Rafe had driven out to try to locate the break—if there actually was one. One way or another, by Miguel's calculations his son should have either called on that cell thing he liked to carry around in his pocket, or driven back by now.

The alternative was that someone was stealing their cattle, an explanation he would rather not entertain. Granted, cattle rustling was not entirely unheard of in this day and age, but he liked his neighbors and there hadn't been a case of rustling in the area for quite some time.

The other alternative was that there were coyotes in the vicinity, hungry ones that could attack a cow and make short work of it. As a boy, he'd once seen a pack of coyotes bring down a full-grown head of cattle and systematically tear the flesh off the poor animal until there were only bones left. The bones were scattered to the extent that it would appear as if the cow had just

vanished. Later, he realized that had he not been looking down on the scene taking place in a gulley, he might
have served as the coyotes' dessert.

Checking his pockets for the keys to his truck,
Miguel thought he heard the front door open and close
again. Miguel Jr. and Ramon were over at Eli's, lend-
ing him a hand with the new quarter horses and, as far
as he knew, Gabe and Alma were working in town as
usual, so that only left one son unaccounted for.

"About time you got back, Raphael," he called out,
making his way to front of the house. "I was all set to
call the sheriff's office and have Alma send out a search
party for you. Did you find the break?" Miguel asked
as he walked into the living room.

Anything else he was about to say faded away as
Miguel stopped in his tracks. Unless his eyes were playing tricks on him, his son was not alone. There was a
very pretty redhead standing beside him.

"No," Rafe answered. "I didn't find the break yet."
*Damn,* he thought. Once he'd stumbled across Valentine and started talking to her, he'd forgotten all about
the break in the fence that he was supposed to be looking for. He flashed his father a semi-apologetic smile.
"But I found her."

Miguel nodded as he made eye contact with the
young woman. He knew the faces of all the people
who lived around here and she *definitely* was not from
around here—although, now that he looked closer, there
was something vaguely familiar about her.

"I see. And she is much more interesting than a break
in the fence," Miguel agreed.

In his early sixties, Miguel Rodriguez was still a virile, powerful man, one who had been extremely handsome in his youth. People told him he still had humor in his dark eyes as well as a certain charm when he smiled.

And he was doing that right now.

Pausing a moment, Miguel glanced toward his son, then back at the attractive young woman he'd brought in with him.

"Since my son seems to have forgotten his manners, let me introduce myself. I am Miguel Rodriguez." He took her hand in his. "Welcome to my humble home," he said just before he bowed from the waist and ever so lightly kissed the hand he was holding, as was the custom of his forefathers. Still bowed, he raised his eyes to hers and asked, "And you are?"

*Intrigued,* Val couldn't help thinking. She'd been born and raised in the land of make believe, accustomed to charm that oozed from the pores of exceptionally handsome men looking to make a name for themselves—or to seduce her for the space of a satisfying liaison or two. Handsome men whose charm—and subsequent nature—was as deep as a puddle on a sidewalk after a light spring shower.

But this Miguel Rodriguez's charm seemed to come as naturally as breathing. Val smiled at the still dark-haired man. He was somewhat shorter than his son, but he appeared to be every bit as powerfully built. Muscles, no doubt, that had come from hard work. She had huge respect for someone like that. Her usual wariness, brought on by years of having to deal with plastic people out only for their own interests and advancement, slipped away like a feather gliding on an unexpected breeze.

"Valentine Jones," she told Rafe's father with a smile.

Miguel's eyes shone with appreciation as they slid over her.

Val caught herself thinking, *Like father, like son* while Miguel told her, "*Con mucho gusto.* That means—"

"I know a little Spanish," she responded. "I know what that means."

"Excellent." Miguel nodded his approval. Slowly releasing her hand, he stepped back. "May I get you something to drink? Perhaps something to eat?"

She liked his generosity. The man was extending his hospitality to her and he had no idea what she was doing there yet.

"No, thank you, Mr. Rodriguez," Val began.

Rafe knew how carried away his father could get, exuding Latin charm from every pore. He came to Val's rescue.

"Val's here on business, Dad," Rafe interrupted before his father could get rolling.

The interested look in Miguel's eyes only grew. "Oh?" His eyes shifted back to the young woman, taking quiet measure of her. "And what business would that be? You cannot be with the bank because all the payments are up to date," he stated just in case this lovely creature with the sharp blue eyes *was* with the establishment that held the mortgage to his property. That would explain why he didn't recognize her. She had to be from out of town. Somewhere up north would be his guess.

"I'm not with the bank," Val confirmed. "I'm in the business of making movies, sir."

Miguel's smile broadened. He slanted a glance toward his son. "Ah, so you have brought me a movie star, Raphael," he said to his son.

Val was quick to correct his mistake—if he'd actually made it. This one, she sensed, was a born flatterer. "I'm not a movie star, Mr. Rodriguez. I work behind the scenes."

*Smooth,* she couldn't help thinking. *And still every bit of a charmer.* She had a feeling that in his day, Miguel Rodriguez had been a force to be reckoned with and that no woman could resist him.

"That is a shame," Miguel told her with genuine feeling. "You should be in front of the camera, not behind one. Come, sit," he encouraged, gesturing toward the oversize tan leather sofa in his living room.

"Thank you."

Walking in front of the older man, Val took a seat on the sofa. Rather than sit beside her, the man she had come to see took a seat on the matching armchair that was positioned kitty-corner to the larger piece of furniture. Looking at him, Val thought of him as a ruler, holding court.

Rafe sat down on the sofa beside her—just close enough to make her aware of his presence even if she wasn't looking directly at him.

"Now then, what can I do for you, Miss—I'm sorry," he apologized, leaning in toward her and creating a very personal space between them. "What did you say your name was again?"

"Valentine Jones," Val repeated. Taking a business card out of the pocket of her jeans, she handed it to the older man.

Miguel glanced at the card, then raised his eyes to hers. She could feel him scrutinizing her. But it wasn't the kind of scrutiny that made her want to squirm. On the contrary, though she wasn't sure just what he was thinking, he made her feel welcomed and right at home. Because of the nature of her work, Val had the ability to adjust to almost any surroundings, but inside, there was always this wariness.

She didn't really feel it this time.

"You know," Miguel told her thoughtfully, "you remind me of someone, the way you hold your head and that beautiful hair of yours. You make me think of an actress. A very pretty lady, but I cannot recall who." He raised his wide shoulders in a helpless shrug, then let them fall. "Getting older has its drawbacks, I am afraid," he confided with a smile. "When I was younger, I would have known immediately."

She knew exactly who he was talking about. It wasn't the first time she'd been told that she reminded a person of someone they had once seen on the screen.

"People say I look like my mother," she told Miguel.

The old man nodded a bit absently. "Many children look like their parents. My daughter, Alma, looks very much like my late wife."

Val had seen photographs of her mother at her age, as well as a few of her movies. She was a dead ringer for her.

"My mother is Gloria Halladay," Val told him, watching his face to see if the name brought any recognition with it.

Miguel's eyes widened with surprise and then infinite pleasure as he put the name to a face. A much-beloved face.

"Yes, of course. Gloria Halladay." There was excitement and a touch of reverence when he said the name. Val found herself instantly liking the man. "I remember seeing her in several movies years ago—I took my wife," he recalled with a fondness enveloping his words. "*Washington's Birthday* was my wife's favorite." Still eying Val, he cocked his head slightly, as another thought occurred to him. "I always thought it was a shame that your mother did not make more comedies. She was very gifted."

Val smiled. "I'll let her know you said so. She'll be very pleased," she told the man. Though she enjoyed her work as a casting director, nothing pleased her mother more than hearing flattering words from a fan. It gave her a sense of continuity as well as bringing back some of the old days.

Miguel nodded thoughtfully and with approval, as if some sort of a bond had just been forged between him and this movie star's daughter.

His eyes swept over the young woman and then his son. The thought occurred to him that Raphael and Gloria Halladay's daughter made a nice couple. A very attractive couple.

He began to wonder what he could do to help them see that.

"So, what is it that I can do for you, Valentine Jones?" he asked warmly.

"She's a location scout, Dad," Rafe interjected. The moment he said it, he realized that his father probably had no idea what that was. He was quick to explain. "That's someone who—"

Miguel waved away the rest of his son's words. "I know what she does, Raphael."

"You do?" This time, it was Val who spoke, surprised that a man from his generation, with no ties to Hollywood, would know what she did for a living.

Miguel inclined his head. "Of course. I know what a scout is and I know what location is. And you said you were with a movie company. That means you are looking for some place suitable to make this movie of yours."

He smiled tolerantly at the two young people. When he was their age, he was certain he was smarter than his father was, too. It was only when he grew older that he realized that perhaps he was not so very smart and his father was not so very dumb.

Miguel's smile deepened fondly. Youth always felt it was smarter than any generation that had come before them.

"It really is not that hard to conclude," he told her. "Continue, please. What is it that you want to say to me?"

Maybe this wasn't going to be so hard after all, Val thought. She was fairly certain that she had won over Raphael, and his father certainly seemed to be reasonable and willing to hear her out.

"Well, Mr. Rodriguez, I think that your ranch would be just perfect for the movie that my boss is getting ready to direct—"

The rest of her sentence was unexpectedly interrupted and then aborted by the loud voice that called out, "Dad, you should see those quarter horses that Eli just got. They— Hello," Mike automatically said, suspending his narrative as he took a look at the stranger sitting in his father's living room. His dark eyes shifted to his father. "Sorry, I didn't know we had company."

Entering behind him, the youngest of the Rodriguez brothers, Ray, came to a sudden halt when Mike stopped moving, all but plowing into his oldest brother. Sidestepping at the last moment, Ray looked to see what had nearly caused the human pileup.

The second he saw the woman on the sofa, a broad grin took possession of his mouth as he tipped the brim of his Stetson in time-honored cowboy fashion.

"Hi," he greeted the woman with enthusiasm. "I'm Ray Rodriguez." His eyes swiftly raced over her as he made a quick, succinct assessment of the woman. "And you are?"

"Overwhelmed," Val readily admitted, looking from one tall, dark and handsome man to another. If she didn't know any better, she would have said she was sitting in the outer room of her mother's casting office when she was casting for the male lead in that last action-adventure movie that had taken place at the turn of the past century.

She turned her attention to the senior Rodriguez. "You've raised a very handsome family, Mr. Rodriguez," she told him. Shifting her attention momentarily back to the two men who had just walked in, she said, "I'm Valentine Jones and I think your ranch and property would be the perfect backdrop for the movie my boss's production company is going to be filming." At this point, her gaze took in all four men, seeking to make a connection with all of them and silently preparing to bring them all on board with this proposal she was about to make.

Mike turned toward his father. The expression on his face was far from pleased. "You didn't say yes, did you, Dad?" he asked.

"I have not had a chance to say very much of anything yet, Miguel." The head of the family looked at the young woman and made the necessary introduction. "This is Miguel Jr., Miss Jones. My oldest."

Val began to rise and extend her hand toward Mike, but before she could say anything, Mike nodded at her curtly, summarily dismissing the offer she had been about to tender.

"If we're voting on this," he told his father, even as he continued looking at the woman, "I vote no."

"Miguel," his father said sharply. "It's only polite to hear the lady out first."

"I don't need to be polite and I don't need to hear what she has to say." The look on Mike's face challenged the interloper in their midst. "They'll come, invade our privacy, disrespect our land, make a mess and then leave." His eyes narrowed dismissively. "Like I said before, I vote no."

Val could feel herself taking umbrage. She'd worked

with this director and his crew a number of times before. They all got along well and had become more like family than merely a crew. She didn't take kindly to this man's careless and dismissive assessment of her "family."

"We clean up after ourselves," Val informed him with a deceptively calm voice. "And your privacy—as well as your land—will be fully respected," she assured him. "Now, would you like to hear why you should say yes?" she asked pleasantly.

Mike was not particularly receptive. No doubt he'd heard stories of what a production crew could be like and didn't want to see that happening to his family's property. "Not particularly," he answered coldly.

"I would," Ray spoke up brightly, flashing a one-thousand-watt smile at her. "By the way, I'm Ray," he said, extending his hand to her. Both he and Mike were still standing where they had entered. "The nice brother," he clarified.

"All my sons are nice," Miguel immediately corrected, then slanted a look at his oldest. "Some are just a little more hotheaded than others."

Val smiled warmly at the patriarch. "I understand," she told Miguel Sr., then appraised the other three men. "I really do. But this is not going to be like some intrusive reality program where the cameramen are going to be following you around, capturing your every movement on film. All we would require from your property would be a few outdoor shots of the ranch house and some panoramic shots of the outlining property." She paused for a moment before adding something that she worried Mike might take exception to. "Our set decorator might want to come and look around inside—"

"And *that's* how it starts," Mike declared as if he had just scored the game-winning point.

Val was not about to give up this easily. "But only to be able to recreate the best parts of your home on a studio set," she insisted, then stressed, "You wouldn't be inconvenienced." Val paused before adding what she hoped was the thing that would win them all over despite Rafe's earlier comment about money not meaning very much to them. "And you would be well compensated for all this."

"Exactly what is 'well compensated' in your book?" Mike asked.

Making the final offer would be the director's decision once he saw her photographs. She didn't want to aim high and then come in with a lower figure. The oldest brother would just use that to try to make his father change his mind.

"Well, just off the top of my head." Val thought for a moment, then quoted what the last person had been paid for the home she had located for the last movie her boss had directed.

No one said a word as the figure sank in.

Ray was the first to say anything, after emitting a long, low whistle in response to the number. "You're kidding."

Mike seemed in complete agreement with the sentiment Ray had just expressed. She *had* to be kidding. No one paid that kind of money just to "borrow" a ranch house. That was the kind of serious money men who were looking to *buy* a ranch house bandied about.

"You're just saying that to get us to agree," Mike accused.

"I'm 'just saying it' because it's true," she informed him. "That was what was paid out for the last house we used on location."

Mike snorted. "Right."

By nature, Rafe was the easygoing one, the one who was neither hotheaded nor sought to be the first to jump into a fray. But he had stood back and listened to just about enough. Since he'd brought the woman to the house to talk to the others, he felt responsible for her. And as the responsible one, he felt obliged to protect her from the likes of someone like his oldest brother, who was acting surly even for Mike.

"Why don't you back off, Mike, and let her talk?" Rafe suggested in a voice that was deceptively calm. "I'm sure there'll be a contract drawn up and if it doesn't have the numbers on it that she's telling us, then Dad doesn't have to sign it and they'll go find their property somewhere else."

Val looked from one member of the family to another. She did *not* want to be the source of discord between these brothers. But she *really* liked what she saw, both the exterior *and* the interior of the place. The more she saw, the more perfect this ranch house seemed to her. She was certain that the director would feel the same way.

"There's another reason to consider agreeing to having my boss film here," she told them. *If at first you don't succeed, try, try again.* She just had to do everything to convince them.

"You having second thoughts about that sum you waved in front of us?" Mike asked.

"No, what I was going to point out is that the crew will be in town for the duration of the shoot, which at this point will be six or eight weeks. That means that for six to eight weeks, they'll be eating here and spending money here. You can't tell me that your town couldn't use that kind of a boost in business, especially in this economy," she said, looking from one man to the other.

*Gotcha,* she thought in satisfaction.

## Chapter Four

"She does have a point," Rafe said, addressing his words to his father.

Their father insisted that they all have an equal voice when it came to matters that affected the ranch, but it was understood among the siblings that it was usually Miguel Sr. who, by mutual agreement, had the absolute final say. They all respected his judgment and knew that he had their best interests, as well as the best interest of the ranch, at heart.

Listening, Miguel nodded, then looked back at the woman who had caused such a stir in their lives with her proposal and, unless he missed his guess, with her very presence. He had seen the look in Raphael's eyes when his son had brought her into the house.

Saw, too, the interest that arose in Ramon's eyes when his youngest son had walked in. Miguel sincerely hoped that there would be no trouble between the brothers because of it. They, like their other brothers, were both handsome young men and while Raphael attracted his fair share of women, it was Ramon, his youngest, who was the playboy, the one who seemed determined to have as much fun as humanly possible, all the while eluding any serious entanglements that might be in the offing.

He wanted to see all of his sons married off, but Ramon gave him the most concern in that department. If any of his sons seemed bent on being an eternal bachelor, it was Ramon.

"I think that we will need to talk this matter over among ourselves," Miguel told the young woman in his usual gentle, quiet cadence. "*If* this man who you are working for does decide that he wants to use our home and land for his…background, you call it?" She nodded in response and he continued, repeating, "If he wants it, *then* we will decide. Until then," Miguel gestured vaguely about the room, indicating that his words referred to anything that they had, "please feel free to make use of our hospitality."

The man seemed incredibly genuine, Val thought as she smiled her gratitude for his understanding. However, she didn't want to take a chance on overstaying her welcome. Rafe's father was right, they needed to talk about this among themselves and either win the dissenting brother over or come to some sort of an understanding they could all agree to. They wouldn't be able to do that if she was standing around within earshot.

"Thank you, but I'd better be on my way," Val told the older man, rising to her feet. Taking the initiative, she shook his hand. "Thank you for your time and I hope we'll be seeing one another again very soon."

Rafe got to his feet, as well. "I'll walk you to your car," he told her. It wasn't an offer so much as a statement.

"Um, Miss Jones—" Ray began, catching her attention as she started to leave.

Val stopped and looked at the youngest member of the family, waiting. "Yes?"

"Who's going to be in this picture of yours?" he asked. It was well-known that his father was only aware of the stars from a bygone era and his brothers weren't interested in the current celebrities who frequented the silver screen, but Ray loved the entertainment world. There were several actresses who had more than captured his admiring attention and he seemed eager to know if any of them would be in town if all this turned out well.

Val didn't bother correcting Ray by saying it wasn't *her* movie. A movie belonged to the producer, to the director, to the writer who had come up with the script and to all the performers who were in it. She was just involved in taking the story and giving it a physical basis where it could unfold.

She thought for a moment, trying to remember the names she'd been told. Coincidentally, her mother had been the casting director for *Cowboys and India,* and her mother had been the one who'd told her who was going to be in this picture.

"Melinda Perkins and Jonathan Kelly are the leading performers," Val answered, remembering. "If you want to know the full cast, I can get that fo—"

"Melinda Perkins?" Ray echoed, his voice rising an octave or so as he repeated the popular actress's name in absolute stunned reverence. "Melinda Perkins is going to be here, standing right *here,* making a movie?" he asked, his breath growing short as his eyes widened with star-struck wonder.

Val's mouth curved as she nodded. "Unless someone's come up with an alternate way to film on location, she'll be here."

"Melinda Perkins, filming right here in Forever," Ray repeated more to himself than to any of his brothers or father, looking even more dazed than he had just a minute ago.

"You already said that," Mike pointed out, shaking his head at what he viewed as juvenile behavior. When he received no response from Ray, other than an utterly goofy look, Mike took the flat of his hand and hit his brother upside his head. "Get a grip, kid," he instructed sharply.

Ray blinked, looking at his oldest brother ruefully, although there were threads of annoyance woven into his expression.

"Miguel," his father said warningly. He himself had never raised a hand to even one of his children and he disapproved of that sort of behavior displayed by any of his offspring.

It was Val who came to Ray's rescue. "Don't feel bad," she told the younger man. "Melinda has that sort of an effect on a lot of people."

Ray flushed slightly, but he was obviously grateful for her defense. He grinned at her. "Mostly men, I'm guessing."

Val didn't answer. Instead, she smiled at him, the

look on her face telling Ray that his guess was absolutely right.

"Miss Jones?" Miguel Sr. broke into the existing conversation. But rather than have her come back to him, the older man crossed over to her. "Are you planning on doing any of your filming in the town itself?" he asked as the thought suddenly occurred to him.

"Most likely," she answered. "I think that the director is going to want to get as much of the local color into this film as possible. That means," she added quickly, "that he's going to want to tap some of the local people to act as extras."

"Extras?" Mike repeated. "Extra what?"

Ray rolled his eyes but Val pretended that this was a perfectly normal question, not one she took for granted.

"Extra people. People who fill in the spaces behind and near the principle actors." She directed her words to the brothers. "You could pick up a little money just by walking around. No dialogue to memorize," she promised.

Miguel rolled her words over in his head. He didn't see a downside to this, but that didn't mean that some of the other people who lived in Forever wouldn't. "I think you might want to present this idea to Miss Joan."

"Miss Joan?" Val echoed a little uncertainly. She glanced at Rafe for an explanation.

He was quick to fill her in. "Miss Joan owns the local—and only—diner. It's also the only restaurant in town. Nothing happens in Forever without her knowing about it. She kind of runs the town," he admitted. "There is a town council in place, but mostly they just listen to what Miss Joan says and go along with it. She's been in Forever as long as anyone can remember."

Out of the corner of her eye, she saw Miguel nodding at his son's words. "So this Miss Joan would be the one to win over," Val said thoughtfully, already planning how to best appeal to the woman she had yet to meet.

"She'd be the one to win over," Mike echoed, nodding his head.

"Okay, I'll keep that in mind," Val replied, adding, "I'll try to be particularly charming. Thank you," she told Miguel warmly, pausing at the door to shake his hand again.

He closed both his hands over her small one and assured her, "My pleasure."

"If you're going to go talk to Miss Joan," Rafe spoke up, joining her at the door, "maybe I should go with you. Always good to have someone from the home team on your side," he added innocently. Having been somewhat undecided when she'd originally told him what she was doing, he'd decided that having Val around might prove to be very interesting. And she was incredibly easy on the eyes, he thought.

"What about the fence?" his father asked belatedly. He liked the idea of his son going into town with this beauty, but he couldn't afford to appear lax.

"The fence isn't going anywhere, Dad," Rafe responded. His thoughts were that he could always look for the break later today, or first thing in the morning. At the moment, this bright, perky woman had captured his full attention.

"Maybe not," his father agreed. "But the cattle apparently are."

Mike frowned, looking from Rafe to his father. "I'll take care of finding the break, Dad," Mike volunteered. "Let Rafe go with her to town." He offered Val a very small smile. "Can't have the lady thinking we're a bunch of rude cavemen now, can we?"

"I wouldn't have thought that anyway," Val assured Mike, then turned toward Rafe and added, "But I wouldn't mind having a guide come with me to make the introductions."

She flashed the smile at him. Rafe found he was having less and less resistance to it every time he saw the smile on her lips.

Miguel could see that he wasn't about to get any decent work out of Gabriel's twin brother today, not judging by the smitten expression on his face.

Seeking to encourage what he felt he saw unfolding before him, Miguel waved Rafe off. "Your brother has a good suggestion. Go, show our guest the way to Miss Joan's."

Rafe had already gone out through the front door. Stopping at the porch, he looked back over his shoulder for a second, nodding his thanks not just to his father, but to Mike, as well. The latter had really surprised him, he had to admit. He was not accustomed to having Mike go out of his way to be nice to him.

"Thanks," Rafe tossed over his shoulder.

But Mike had already left the room, going to the

kitchen to grab a bite of something to eat before he headed out again.

It was his father who called after Rafe, promising, "Do not worry, I will tell him that you are grateful."

This time, Rafe nodded his thanks to his father.

Val followed Rafe down the front steps and toward where they had parked their individual vehicles. "I don't think your brother likes me very much," Val confided once they were clear of the house.

"That's just Mike being Mike," Rafe told her. "My older brother tends to be a little standoffish with strangers."

"I would have thought your father would be guilty of that, not your older brother. You know, older generation, my being an outsider, that sort of thing," she explained. Val stopped by her CRV. "Instead, your dad seems to be a very warm, friendly man."

Rather than going to his Jeep, Rafe paused by her light blue vehicle. "He always has been where a pretty woman was concerned," he told her.

For a moment, the words just seemed to hang in the air between them. And then she laughed.

"I think you're a little confused," she told him. "I'm supposed to be flattering you to get you to go along with my boss's production company using your ranch for the movie, not the other way around."

Val's amused smile rose up into her eyes, all but mesmerizing him. Rafe had never believed that eyes could actually smile before.

He did now.

"Didn't see any harm in stating the truth," he told her. She probably thought that was a line. The woman was from Hollywood, which undoubtedly made her see everything with a jaded point of view, not to mention that she was probably immune to any kind of a compliment, genuine or not. He cleared his throat and said, "If you wait a second, I'll go start up my Jeep and you can follow me into town."

Val looked over her shoulder. The house was some distance away now, but she could still make out Miguel Rodriguez. The man was standing on the porch, observing them. When he saw her looking in his direction, he smiled and waved at her.

Val waved back. "You're sure I'm not taking you away from anything?" she asked Rafe.

"Just from driving around, looking for that damn break in the fence. Trust me, going into town and introducing you to Miss Joan is a much better proposition. Besides, Mike's really better at that sort of thing, anyway. It's like he's got a sixth sense when it comes to that. He's a natural-born rancher."

She read things into his endorsement, things he wasn't saying. "And you're not?"

He wouldn't exactly rule himself out completely, but there was a big difference between him and Mike when it came to ranching. "Not as good as Mike is," he assured her.

Thanks to her parents bringing her onto the set before she was even walking, as well as having to deal with all sorts of people in her chosen profession, she'd gotten very good at being able to read people, be it the

inflection in their voice or the body language they unwittingly used.

She studied him now for a few moments before asking, "Does that bother you?"

He shrugged. "Not particularly." He wondered if that
made him lacking in some way. "I'm still not sure what
my niche is, anyway. But I do know that Mike's the real
rancher—just like Eli," he added belatedly. Recently
married to his childhood sweetheart, Eli had great plans
for his small ranch. Plans that including gaining more
property as time went on.

His money was on Eli. If anyone could make that
ranch of his flourish, it was Eli.

Her eyebrows drew together as she looked at Rafe
quizzically. "Eli?"

He nodded. "He has his own spread just on the other
side of this one. You might want to check it out, as well.
The ranch house is a lot smaller than ours, though," he
warned.

Val shook her head. "I don't need to check it out,"
she told him, although she appreciated the invitation.
"Your ranch house is exactly what we're looking for."
She thought of what he'd said to her before, that they all
voted on matters concerning their property. How many
of these people was she going to have to win over? "I
never asked," she recalled. "How many are there in your
family, anyway?"

"Well, you already met Mike and Ray—and me,"
Rafe added with a smile. "And I told you about Eli.
That leaves Alma and Gabe," he told her. "They both

work for the sheriff," he confided. Having a feeling he knew why she was asking how many siblings he had, he added, "Alma's pretty easygoing and so's Gabe. He's my twin and more or less thinks the same way I do."

"You're a twin?" she asked, surprised. With all the people her mother dealt with, Val couldn't remember ever meeting a set of twins before. She cocked her head, studying Rafe again, looking at him in a brand new light. He resembled the two brothers she'd just met and she could seem a family resemblance between Rafe and his father. What was it like to have someone else he knew walking around with his face?

"Do people get the two of you confused with each other?" she asked. She didn't know how she'd feel having a twin. She did know that while she enjoyed certain aspects of being an only child, she also wished she had at least one sibling, if not a couple, to share things with, especially when she was growing up.

Rafe shook his head. "Not really, except for my mother. But that was more of a name thing than a face thing," he explained. He could see that his explanation just confused her further. "When my mother was yelling for one of us to listen to her, she'd go through the whole list of names before she got to the right one—and she didn't always," he added. "Can't tell you how many times she called me Alma."

"Well, you certainly don't look like an Alma," Val assured him with a laugh.

He grinned. "Thanks. We're not identical," he said, then belatedly, in case she thought he was still talking about his sister, he quickly clarified the point by saying, "Gabe and me. He was born first by three minutes. And he's taller by an inch, but I'm better looking," he deadpanned.

She didn't bother to hide her good-natured grin. "I see."

Val wasn't sure if he was actually kidding or not, but she did feel laughter bubbling up inside of her. If he *wasn't* kidding, then she'd hurt his feelings by laughing and she really didn't want to do that. Most men, she'd come to learn, had extremely fragile egos. Even her late husband had had his limits and he'd been, in her exceptionally young opinion at the time, pretty near perfect.

Doing her best to hide her amusement, Val asked, "Does he think that, too? That he's the handsomer one of the two of you?"

"Well, Gabe knows he's taller," Rafe said. "But he probably thinks he's the better-looking one. However, he doesn't usually look into mirrors much," Rafe responded, tongue in cheek.

"Uh-huh."

If the man looked anything like Rafe, Val thought, then it was safe to assume that he was equally drop-dead gorgeous.

Glancing back at the house, she could see that Miguel Sr. was still standing in the doorway and would most likely remain there until they—or at least she—finally got into the car and left.

Deciding to oblige him—it was time to get going anyway—Val made sure she had Miguel's attention and waved at the man, then got into her vehicle.

She rolled down her window and said to Rafe, "We'd better be on our way before your father changes his mind about being able to spare you."

Did she think he was that necessary to the operation of the ranch? Or was she just pulling his leg, making a droll comment, he wondered.

In any case, Rafe felt she might have a point about his father changing his mind. He did that on occasion and God knew there was always something to do on the ranch, despite the fact that these days, they hired on part-time help whenever it was necessary. And the few times that they had run out of things that needed attending to on their ranch, there was always Eli. Eli never turned down an offer from one of them to help around his ranch. He was always grateful to have a hand or two volunteering to help him. If nothing else, the price was right.

"It'll just take me a minute to get the Jeep started," he promised. He probably didn't need to tell her that, he thought, since she'd already been privy to the way his vehicle had acted up previously. It had all but coughed its way into service before he was able to lead her back to the ranch house.

Val nodded. "There's no hurry," she assured him. "I'm actually ahead of schedule. I didn't expect to find a place to use so soon," she told him. "Not that I'm count-ing my chickens before they hatch," she added quickly. She didn't want to come across as being too confident. She'd learned from experience that men didn't like women who came on overly confident.

"Maybe not chickens," he agreed good-naturedly

as he walked toward his vehicle. "But I think you can count your ranchers before they hatch," he told her, punctuating his statement with a wink before he walked off.

## Chapter Five

Being on the receiving end of Rafe's exceedingly sexy wink, Val couldn't help thinking that her mother might be interested in meeting this man.

Rafe Rodriguez was as handsome as any man who had come through the door of Gloria Halladay's casting office and when he winked like that, he had the definite makings of a heartbreaker. There was no doubt in her mind that Rafe could very easily create mini tidal waves inside the average red-blooded female's stomach.

Not to mention that the man had that little extra "something." Good-looking men were pretty much a dime a dozen where she came from, but men who had something special that set them apart, who had that elusive electric spark some called "chemistry," those kind of men were not as common as some people might have thought.

Her mother, she was fairly certain, would have snapped Rafe up in a heartbeat and offered to give him acting lessons if he felt unequal to the task. What Rafe had couldn't be bought or taught. It was either there or it wasn't. In Rafe's case, it was most definitely "there."

Val found herself thinking about Rafe the entire time she followed him to town and Miss Joan's diner.

"You ever think of becoming an actor?" was the first thing she asked Rafe when they arrived at their destination and she got out of her CRV.

She'd parked alongside of his Jeep and in front of a weather-beaten diner that looked as if it was as much a part of the terrain as the tumbleweeds that were languidly chasing one another in the distance.

"Say what?" Rafe asked, certain that he hadn't heard her question correctly.

"Did you ever think of becoming an actor?" Val repeated.

Okay, there was nothing wrong with his hearing, just her thought process. Rafe shook his head at the notion. As far as he was concerned, acting wasn't an actual *job*, it was an indulgence. The way he saw it, acting was carrying childhood games of make-believe too far. The idea of being an actor amused him and he could just hear what his brothers would have had to say about *that*.

All except Ray, of course, who probably secretly would have really liked the idea—especially if it involved him in some way.

"Can't say the thought ever crossed my mind," he said out loud, adding, "Doesn't exactly seem like an honest way to earn a living, standing around and saying words someone else put in my mouth." Rafe looked at her for a long moment, wondering what had prompted her to ask him something like that. "Why?"

She had a feeling that Rafe might have gotten the wrong idea about how she meant the question. He might even take it to mean that she was interested in him—and she wasn't. Because she'd been that route. Been ultimately hurt taking that route, and once was more than enough for her.

"No reason," she told him casually. "I guess I just asked out of habit. Where I come from," she explained, "every second person wants to be either an actor or a screenwriter and I was just wondering if either of those two occupations appealed to you."

Rafe laughed at the mere suggestion of the possibility. "I'm used to working with my hands," he told her, then added as an afterthought, "And sweating. Don't think you'd have any use for a sweaty actor."

He meant it as a joke, but she was looking at him seriously, evaluating his potential. The camera would love him, Val decided.

"Sweaty's not really a bad thing anymore," she told Rafe. "Movies have gotten a lot more real than they used to be."

In response, his shrug was casual, almost careless. "I wouldn't know. Like I said, I don't watch too many movies. Now Ray, he's the one to talk to about movies if you want a decent conversation on the subject. He's really into that kind of stuff."

Ray seemed nice, but she didn't want to talk about Ray. She wanted to talk about *him*.

"You don't even like action movies?" Val found that hard to believe. All guys liked action movies. It was built into their DNA.

For a second he thought about just saying yes and letting it go at that. But that would be lying, and as a rule, he didn't. So he shook his head in response. "Sorry. If anything, I like my action up close and personal."

Amusement curved her mouth. *I just bet you do.* An image of a half-naked Rafe, lost in the throes of lovemaking, suddenly flashed through her mind out of nowhere.

Stunned, Val was quick to bank it down before it got too involved. She *really* didn't need to be distracted like that, especially not this early in her dealings with the local people.

Still, she couldn't resist asking, "Hence the sweating?"

His smile was just the slightest bit lopsided as he answered, "Something like that."

Why that would suddenly make her feel so unduly warm wasn't something Val had the time or the energy to explore right at this moment. She had a potential town leader to charm.

Val took a few steps toward the diner before she stopped for a second.

Because he thought she was going to walk up the three steps and go straight into the diner, Rafe had to stop short to narrowly avoid colliding with her. That would have made twice in one day that they would have made total-body contact and while that sort of thing *definitely* had its appeal as far as he was concerned, Rafe didn't want the woman thinking that he was crowding her—literally.

So, after quickly regaining his bearings, Rafe asked her, "Something wrong?"

Val was no longer an intern nor an untried novice

with the production company, feeling her way around unfamiliar territory. She'd been with Jim Sinclair and his crew for over three years now. Even so, she still didn't want to take a chance and blow it.

She could feel it in her gut—this *was* the perfect place for the story they were going to be filming. Oh, she knew that there were other places that could lend themselves to this story just as well, but that would require a concentrated effort. It would mean starting from scratch and she didn't feel like scratching, not when the perfect setting was right in front of her.

But in order for this to happen, she sensed that she really had to win over this Miss Joan the Rodriguez men seemed so sold on. And, if she was about to beard the lioness in her den, she wanted to know what sort of lioness she was up against.

"What's this Miss Joan like?" she asked Rafe.

Rafe thought for a moment before he spoke. He didn't want to make a mistake and give Val the wrong impression of the woman the whole town loved and respected for as many different reasons as there were people living in Forever.

"She likes to think she's tough, but she looks out for everyone around here. Miss Joan keeps us in line and pretty grounded. Someone needs a little extra money to tide them over, she slips it to them quietly. If someone has no place to stay, she'll take them in until they're back on their feet. Miss Joan doesn't like calling attention to her softer side, but it's there nonetheless. In spades," he assured her, then, as if to add extra credence to his words, he added, "My sister's married to her stepson."

"So that means you have an 'in' with her," Val assumed, really happy that she'd thought to bring him along with her.

"Everyone's got an 'in' with Miss Joan," he countered. "They just happen to be different kinds of 'ins.'"

Val considered his answer. She supposed that sounded reasonable. "Just as long as I'm not dealing with Meryl Streep in *The Devil Wears Prada*," she said wryly.

Rafe blinked. Was that someone he was supposed to know? "Who?"

For a second, she'd forgotten that Rafe had an entirely different frame of reference than she did. And if she had to explain the meaning of the comment, it lost its meaning and really wasn't worth it.

"Never mind," she said, dismissing her flippant statement. "Any words of advice?"

Nothing really occurred to him. He thought back to what his mother always used to tell them. "Just be yourself."

Val had to press her lips together to suppress the laugh that rose in her throat. What he'd just said sounded suspiciously like the "words to live by" in every Disney movie she'd seen as a child.

"Well, I suppose I can do that better than anyone," she murmured under her breath.

Val realized she was uncharacteristically nervous and had no idea why. With effort, she pushed those feelings to the background. Squaring her shoulders, she pulled open the door and walked into the diner.

She'd assumed, because she'd taken for granted that there would probably be at least two women behind the long counter, that she would have to ask Rafe which of the women was Miss Joan. But the moment she entered the diner, she realized that wouldn't be necessary. There were three women wearing uniforms in the diner, two behind the counter and one on the floor. The latter was bringing an order over to three men at one of the booths along the wall.

It wasn't age that gave away the owner of the diner—one of the women behind the counter appeared older than the woman on the floor. It was the air with which she carried herself.

Miss Joan moved like a queen amid her well-loved subjects.

Walking up to the woman removing three plates of hot stew from her tray and placing each before one of the men seated at the booth, Val smiled at her and politely asked, "Miss Joan?"

Amber eyes with flecks of green rose to look at her face. There was a flash of interest in them as the older woman took measure of her.

"Yes?"

Val gave Miss Joan her best disarming smile as she introduced herself. Inwardly, Val braced herself for anything, since, Rafe's assessment of the diner's owner not withstanding, she really didn't know what to expect.

"I'm Valentine Jones."

"Was that your mama's idea, or your daddy's?" Miss

Joan asked, putting down the last order of stew. She took a step back as she gave the young woman with Rafe her full attention.

The woman had lost her already, Val thought though she did her best not to appear bewildered.

"Excuse me?"

"Was that your mama's idea, or your daddy's?" Miss Joan repeated.

It didn't make any more sense to her the second time around than it had the first. "Was *what* my mother's idea or my father's?"

"Your given name," Miss Joan said patiently. "Did your mama think you were her little Valentine or was that what your daddy thought?"

Val was about to say that she had no idea whose idea it was, but then a faraway memory from her childhood seemed to come out of nowhere. She was on her father's lap and he was reading something to her out of the Sunday comics. Something to do with Valentine's Day. "Bet you didn't know that was why we called you Valentine," she could almost *hear* him saying.

"Why, Daddy?" she remembered asking.

"Because the first time I ever laid eyes on you," he'd told her, "I just fell in love with you. I told your mom that you were like my own personal little Valentine from heaven."

The sliver of a memory brought a smile to her lips as she relished it.

"My father's," she answered in almost a whisper. Then, raising her eyes to the woman, she repeated what she'd just said, more loudly this time. And with plea-sure. "I'd forgotten all about that until just now."

Miss Joan nodded, as if she'd expected her question to unearth a long-lost memory. The ghost of a smile on her lips was one tinged with satisfaction.

"Why don't you two take a seat at the counter and then you can tell me what it is you want to ask." The last part of Miss Joan's statement was addressed to her, Val realized. How did the woman know that she had something to ask her?

Unable to answer that for herself, she glanced quiz-zically at Rafe. The latter merely smiled at her in re-sponse. The expression on his face seemed to say, "I told you so."

"You boys okay?" Miss Joan asked the three men she'd just served.

All three responded in a disjointed cacophony that just amounted to different forms of affirmative re-sponses. The men made no secret of their apparent in-terest in the stranger that Rafe Rodriguez had brought into their midst.

Pretty women never went unappreciated.

"Don't stare so hard, Howard. Your eyes are liable to fall right out of your head," Miss Joan warned just before she turned her back on the trio.

Weaving her way through the crowded diner, she made her way to the counter. Pausing, she took assess-ment of the seating. There were a couple of single seats available, but no two were together.

"Billy, Travis," she called out. When the two men looked at her, she waved toward the empty stools. "Why don't you boys do me a favor and just scoot yourselves over to the left some, so that Rafe here can have a seat next to his lady?" It was phrased as a request, but they knew it was more than that.

As the two men abruptly rose and silently shifted over to the left to accommodate Miss Joan's "request," Val felt the need to correct the woman's mistaken impression of the situation.

"Oh, I'm not Rafe's 'lady,'" Val told her.

Miss Joan slanted her a look and grunted "Uh-huh," as if she was just humoring her. The woman's expression was completely unfathomable.

Val began to reiterate her denial, then stopped. She had the feeling that doing so would only make things that much worse, that any protest would somehow just make a case for the other side that much stronger.

This wasn't grade school, she reminded herself. No adamant denials were necessary, just a simple statement of fact before dropping the matter was all that was required. The woman could think whatever she wanted to. It didn't make any difference. She was here for a far more important reason than clarifying her status. She was here to hopefully get the woman's blessings and film Sinclair's movie here.

Val knew that if Rafe's father allowed them the use of his ranch and this Miss Joan put the kibosh on the crew filming within the town proper, the production crew could always find a way around that. But she also knew that it would be far easier—and to everyone's mutual benefit—if she could get the queen bee's approval to go ahead with using the town itself—and its citizens—in the movie.

"Can I get you two anything?" Miss Joan was asking, looking exclusively at her even though she'd used the word "two."

She needed to get the small talk out of the way, Val thought.

"Water will be fine," she told the owner of the diner.

"Water's to wash with," Miss Joan told her dismissively. She tried again. "So, what'll it be? Lemonade? Iced tea? Coffee?"

Because she had a feeling that if she didn't select *something* the woman would just doggedly keep giving her choices—or worse, become insulted, Val gravitated to the first choice she'd been offered.

"The lemonade sounds good."

"The lemonade *is* good," Miss Joan confirmed. She looked at Rafe and raised one carefully penciled-in eyebrow. "Two?" she asked.

"Two," he agreed.

Miss Joan's thin lips curved in approval ever so slightly. "Be right back," she promised.

Entering the kitchen through double swinging doors, she retreated to retrieve a pitcher of the promised lemonade.

As she sat there at the counter, Val could swear that she felt every pair of eyes in the diner were on her. It wasn't a matter of vanity. She knew she looked like her mother and that her mother had been considered beautiful at this stage of her career, but that had nothing to do with this.

Leaning into Rafe, she asked, "I take it you don't get too many people coming through Forever."

Rafe couldn't help grinning. "None that look like you."

She was more than accustomed to hearing compliments, when they were merited and especially when they weren't. It was all part of the game. Compliments were tendered with an endgame in mind.

The endgame being seduction.

She was also accustomed to blocking compliments, to deftly avoiding getting caught up in any flowery displays of rhetoric intended to get her ensnared in a web. But Rafe had said what he'd said without an obvious endgame. He'd given her a compliment, she realized, because he thought it was true.

Which would explain why she could feel herself blushing.

Deliberately avoiding making any eye contact with him, she turned on the swivel counter stool to face the people in the diner. She noticed that more than half of them were men. Taking that into account, she dug out her one-thousand-watt smile.

"Hi," she said, addressing all of them at the same time. "I'm Val Jones," she told them, thinking that it might be prudent not to use her whole name at this time and thus avoid the possibility of getting asked the same question that the diner's owner had put to her.

A chorus of "hellos" greeted her. That and one tall, hulking wrangler in worn-out boots and even more worn jeans strode over to her.

"You looking for a good time, Val Jones?" he asked,

leaning over her stool and giving the impression of crowding her. "'Cause I can give you a better one than he can," he assured her, jerking a dismissive thumb in Rafe's direction.

Before she could think of a way to answer his statement that wouldn't create a problem rather than avoid one, she heard someone behind her speak up first.

A sense of relief washed over her as she heard Miss Joan's voice.

"Why don't you go and sit down, Emmett?" It was more of an order than a question. Turning, Val saw that Miss Joan had returned with the pitcher of lemonade and took charge of the situation. "She's not interested in having any kind of a time with you, good or bad, so my advice to you is to stop making a fool of yourself and just go sit down," she told the lumbering wrangler with finality.

# Chapter Six

Turning back to the twosome she'd placed at the counter, Miss Joan noted that Rafe was no longer seated but on his feet, no doubt ready to defend the young woman he'd brought with him.

For as long as she could remember, even when he was a little guy, Rafe had always been slow to anger. But once there, he was a force to be reckoned with. The fact that Emmett had fifty pounds on the Rodriguez boy was not a deterrent.

"Down, boy," Miss Joan said affectionately, lightly patting Rafe's chest to get him to sit back down on the stool again. "Confrontation's been averted. Nobody wants to watch you messing up that pretty face of yours," the older woman said matter-of-factly as she made her way back behind the counter again.

Taking two tall glasses out from beneath the counter, she placed them before Val and Rafe and filled each one with lemonade. Finished, she set the pitcher down and waited.

"Well, take 'em." She gestured toward the untouched

glasses of lemonade. "The glasses aren't going to walk up to you."

They did as she said. Miss Joan waited until they'd had a chance to sample the lemonade, then focused her attention pointedly on the newcomer. "Now, then, what is it that I can do for you?"

It made Val a little uneasy that the woman had worded it just that way. It was as if Miss Joan was looking right into her thoughts. "I represent Sinclair Productions," Val began. "That's a—"

"—movie company," Miss Joan concluded for her. "Yeah, I know." She saw the surprised look on Rafe's face. "What, you thought I didn't know what that was?" she questioned, looking from Val back to Rafe. "I read *People* magazine," she informed them with just a hint of indignation. "I know that there's a world outside of Forever and I keep up on it." Shifting her eyes back exclusively to Val, she encouraged the young woman to, "Go on."

Val continued with her pitch, wondering how much she actually needed to say and how much Miss Joan already knew. Did that mean the woman had already made up her mind and this was just to see what she might have to say to sway the decision her way?

Whatever the game, she'd play it as long as the outcome was what she needed it to be. Maybe this was the way the woman entertained herself.

"They're going to be filming a romantic comedy about a woman going to a dude ranch to get over her divorce. The story is set in the 1960s—"

"And you think we're old-fashioned looking enough

to serve as the movie's location?" Miss Joan guessed, interrupting.

Most of the time, when she dealt with home owners and the heads of town councils in some of the smaller towns that Jim tended to favor when he was shooting his films, she had to literally explain everything to the people from the moment she began. This woman was apparently far more savvy that the average person she encountered, Val thought. Miss Joan obviously had a handle on how a production company operated.

It made her wonder just exactly what the woman had done for a living before she'd come to live here. She had assumed that Miss Joan was a native to the area, but maybe she'd been wrong.

More than anything, she wished she could read the woman's expression, but right now, she hadn't a clue. Crossing her fingers, Val continued.

"Not exactly old-fashioned," she tactfully amended. "Forever has the warm, homey feel that Sinclair Productions is always looking for."

"Very diplomatic." Miss Joan nodded her approval, adding, "You've got a real way with words, girl. So," she said, moving the conversation along, "why are you looking to talk to me?"

"Well, if Rafe's father agrees, we'll be using his ranch in the movie, but we'd like to do some background filming here in the town and maybe use some of the local people for extras."

"Extra what?" Someone in the diner called out the question.

He was quickly answered by someone else in the

diner. "Extra people, you dummy," the man told him condescendingly. "Don't you know anything?"

The sound of a chair scraping along the black-and-white tiled floor was heard as the first man challenged the second. "I know enough not to call someone I work with every day a dummy."

"That's 'cause I'm not the dummy," the second man snapped.

The voices grew louder—and uglier. "You saying that I am?"

"Excuse me," Miss Joan politely said to Val.

Like a winged fury on a mission, Miss Joan moved from behind the counter to the feuding two men. She got between them, her expression reproving despite the fact that each of the men was at least twice her size. They both loomed over her like storybook giants on the verge of battle.

The woman looked small, Val couldn't help thinking. It occurred to her that a stick of dynamite might look small, but could still easily take down a tall tree with no effort.

"You two lunkheads want to be banned from my establishment for life, just keep this up," Miss Joan warned them.

The men glared at one another, then ever so slowly, their expressions turned contrite as they addressed the woman between them.

"Sorry, Miss Joan," the two hulking wranglers all but chorused together.

Satisfied that the fuse had been extinguished for now, Miss Joan returned to Val and Rafe.

"You were saying?" she prompted Val as if nothing had happened.

Val looked at her with new respect. Rafe had not exaggerated about the woman being in charge here. "I wanted to know if it would be all right with you and the rest of the town council, or whoever it is that rules on these things, for the production company to film here."

Miss Joan didn't answer immediately. Just as Val was about to restate her question, the woman finally spoke. "Well, I don't see the harm in it," she allowed. "And these film people, they'll be staying here in town for a bit, right?"

"Absolutely. We're bringing in trailers," Val explained in case the woman was going to ask her where everyone intended to stay. She was fairly certain that she hadn't seen a hotel in the town—at least not so far. And if there was one, she knew it wouldn't be able to accommodate all the people needed to make this movie.

"I suspect that they'll be needing to eat, to buy supplies, unwind at the local establishment, right?" Miss Joan asked, quietly studying her expression.

"Absolutely," Val assured her with feeling. She cocked her head, watching Miss Joan's face. "So you don't have any objections?"

"As long as these Hollywood people of yours mind their manners, I don't see a problem. Having them in town's fine with me." Miss Joan's thin lips curved in the smallest of smiles. "Now that that's out of the way, what can I get you?"

Val looked at the tall glass before her. She'd only consumed a little less than half its contents. As far as she was concerned, this was more than adequate. "You brought us these." Val nodded at her glass, indicating that the lemonade was more than sufficient to satisfy her needs.

"That was to drink, not to eat," Miss Joan pointed out. "I realize you don't put all that much into your mouth, judging by the size of that waist of yours," the diner owner said, glancing at Val's flat waistline, "but you have to eat *something*. You might as well have that 'something' here," Miss Joan speculated.

"I actually have a very healthy appetite," Val protested. She knew that it had to look as if she was constantly dieting—but she wasn't. She ate more than her fair share. The thing of it was, she had the metabolism of an overactive hummingbird.

"You lend it out to someone?" Rafe asked her, his eyes slowly traveling over the length of her.

They didn't believe her, not that she could actually blame them. At her heaviest, she'd weighed in at one-twenty. These days the scale only reached up to one-twelve and that was after she gorged herself.

"All right," Val said gamely. "Let me see one of your menus."

Miss Joan obliged, presenting her with a laminated double-sided page. Turning toward Rafe, she asked, "You don't need one, do you?"

He shook his head. "Not unless you changed it recently."

Miss Joan smiled, then quoted one of her favorite sayings. "If it ain't broke, don't fix it." She'd been using the same menu now for the past couple of years and business was just as booming now as it ever had been. "The only thing different is that we have some really good pastries these days, thanks to Gabe's fiancée," she interjected for Val's benefit. "But there's no sense trying to put that down on a menu 'cause Angel changes it every day, making whatever it is that moves her at the time." Miss Val leaned in and lowered her voice. "She's also helping me keep Eduardo in line," the older woman confided, nodding her head toward the kitchen. "The old coot's stopped talking about retiring and leaving me stranded ever since I hired on Angel back in early December."

Pausing for effect, Miss Joan smiled triumphantly. "She and Gabe'll be getting married soon, I expect." That had been for Val's benefit. And then she looked at Rafe. "That only leaves three of you Rodriguez boys at home," the woman pointed out as if it wasn't something that Rafe was keenly aware of. Miss Joan's amber eyes shifted back to Val. "Made up your mind yet, honey?"

Maybe it was her imagination but she could have sworn that the way the woman asked the question, she wasn't really talking about lunch.

Be that as it may, Val was not about to get herself caught up in something that she had no intention of taking part in. Her mother and her mother's friends had already tried to get her to begin going out socially again. But anything other than a girls' night out was still out of the question as far as she was concerned.

Maybe it always would be.

All she knew was that she was not about to dive into the deep end of the pool again. Not even with a mask and water wings to protect her. One broken heart was more than enough for her.

"I think I'll have the chicken enchilada," Val decided, handing the menu back to Miss Joan.

"Just one?" Miss Joan asked, accepting the menu.

Most likely she could do justice to at least two enchiladas, but she didn't want to commit herself to more than one until she knew what it tasted like. She could eat one no matter what it tasted like. Two, however, would be pushing it.

"For starters," Val answered pleasantly.

"But you could eat more," Miss Joan pressed.

"I could," Val allowed.

Miss Joan smiled her approval. "Good. That's what I like to hear."

"WHERE ARE YOU staying?" Rafe asked.

It was the tail end of the day, one they had spent together. After lunch at the diner, he had taken her around to see the rest of the town. He'd introduced her to the people he felt she might want to meet and would want to possibly introduce to her boss once the deal to film here had been finalized all around.

The idea of that taking place began to fill him with a degree of enthusiasm. It would definitely be a change of pace for the town, not to mention that it meant he'd be able to see Val for a while. The possibility of that made him smile even more. A sense of anticipation began to take hold of him.

After they'd finished with the town, Rafe had also acted as her tour guide for the outlining areas, as well, bringing her to the reservation where Joe Lone Wolf, one of the deputies who worked with Alma, had been born. The tour was a deliberately slow process that allowed her to absorb the majesty of the remote area.

He enjoyed watching the way her face lit up when she took in a particularly breathtaking view. Val genuinely reacted to the land the way he did and he particularly liked that.

But now the sun had begun to set and although he had a feeling that she was trying desperately not to show it, Val was getting tired. With that in mind, he'd taken her back to the diner—and her CRV—and insisted on buying her dinner, which he managed to do over her protest.

When they came back into the diner, Miss Joan had greeted her as if she were an old friend rather than someone she'd met just that morning.

After being given the full tour and enjoying the local color, Val had to admit that part of her could see the very real appeal of living in a place like Forever.

But she shut away that thought almost the moment it popped into her head. This was a nice place to visit, but she belonged in the hustle and bustle of a place like Hollywood, not in a place where, if you listened really hard, you could hear the cacti growing. She needed excitement more than she needed tranquility.

"Why?" she asked him, referring to Rafe's question as to where she was spending the night. "Are you looking to get yourself invited over?"

The second the words were out of her mouth, she realized that she'd attributed traits to him that were unwarranted. He hadn't hit on her once today, being nothing but the perfect gentleman, even when he'd fallen on top of her, saving her from the bull. She had to admit that it had caused her to wonder if there was something wrong with her, but that was just her insecurity.

"Sorry," she apologized. "I'm afraid I was just thinking about the guys back home. They tend to be a little, let's say, *pushy.*"

He couldn't say that he blamed those men. The woman next to him not only had a gorgeous face, but she had a killer body, as well, the kind that could make many a man sit up and beg. She was probably accustomed to that sort of behavior and he didn't want to get lumped in with a crowd of other men. He wanted, for whatever short duration, to stand out from the crowd. The crowd of men who called her and insisted on leaving text messages. He'd heard her phone signaling her all day.

"Wasn't trying to be pushy or get invited over," he told her quietly. "I was just going to offer to accompany you there and make sure you got in safely. And," he admitted, "to be honest I was also kind of curious who you were staying with."

"Staying with?" Val echoed, slightly bewildered.

"Yeah. Forever doesn't have a hotel or motel, although there's been some talk that they just might start building one for visitors. But I didn't see a trailer when I took you out on that tour of the area."

She laughed, going for the sidebar first. "I'd suggest that your town council give the okay to start building fast. Film groupies tend to like to visit where a movie's been filmed."

His eyes widened. She could see that even in the growing darkness. "You're kidding."

"Nope," she answered, drawing an invisible cross over her heart. "You'd be surprised how loyal some movie fans can be. If the hero kisses the heroine by that tree," she pointed to one in the distance, "they'll want to come here and carve their initials in it. As for where I'm staying," she continued, "it's a hotel clear in the next town." Mission Ridge, she thought it was called.

"That's fifty miles away," he pointed out.

She nodded. "I know. That didn't sound like much this morning when I started driving around, looking," Val admitted. "But now, I know it's going to feel more like five-hundred miles than fifty."

Rafe made her an offer that he felt was only polite. "You could stay at our place if you'd like," he told the young woman.

She smiled. "You mean stay at the Old Homestead?" she teased. "Tempting as that sounds, I think that just might give your Miss Joan a bit too much to talk about. She already looks as if she's envisioning the two of us being an 'item,'" Val replied, using the old-fashioned word she felt would probably come more easily to the other woman's tongue.

Rafe supposed that he could see her point. He didn't want to seem as if he was pressuring her, he was just looking out for her. "If it made you feel better, you could stay at Alma's."

Her eyes narrowed as she absorbed what he was

telling her. "You're volunteering your sister's place?" she asked. And then humor curved the corners of her mouth. "I don't know if she'd take kindly to that. Besides, didn't you tell me that Alma recently married Miss Joan's stepson?"

"Yeah, I did. She did," he added. "But he's cool. He won't say anything to Miss Joan, especially if you don't want him to." He put a hand on her shoulder, intending to create a bond to get his point across. However, he could feel something else happening, as well, something transcending a mere bond. He tried to put it out of his mind as he told her, "Hospitality's important to us out here and besides, you look like you might just be too tired to drive. I counted five yawns in the past hour and I sure as hell hope it's because you're tired and not because of the company you're keeping."

She laughed softly then and the sound went straight to his gut. "Definitely not the company," she assured him. She pressed her lips together as she thought over his offer. It definitely had appeal. "You sure your father won't mind if I turn up on his doorstep?"

"What he'd mind is if I let you drive your vehicle all the way back to Mission Ridge in your present tired condition. Even with my following you, it's still asking for trouble," he pointed out.

She thought about it for a moment. She loved being independent, but she had to admit that he did have a point. She had stayed out longer than she'd intended. She'd gotten caught up in the conversation and the stories he had to tell. It had made her lose track of time and now she really did feel rather wiped out.

Although Val was fairly sure that she wouldn't drive into some ditch, there was no sense in taking chances. The cemetery was filled with people who didn't think that they would fall asleep on the road.

"Okay, if you're absolutely positive that your father won't mind, we can go back to your family's ranch."

Rafe grinned at her. "Dad won't mind, but out of curiosity, why didn't you pick Alma's place?"

There was a very simple reason for that. "Because, according to what Miss Joan said, Alma and her husband haven't been married all that long and newlyweds don't need to have a third wheel hanging around them."

He hadn't thought about it that way. "Maybe you're right," he agreed for form's sake. He was actually thinking that he was glad she'd decided to come back to the ranch with him. "Tell you what," he began. "Why don't we leave your vehicle here and I'll drive us to the ranch?"

"Leave it here?" she repeated, glancing at the CRV uncertainly. She didn't like the idea of leaving a vehicle unattended overnight. Where she came from, that was how cars got stripped.

"Sure. Nobody'll bother it," he assured her, "and since you're coming to our ranch, I'll be there in the morning to bring you back to town—and to your car. There's no point in both of us driving there and back—and there's always that danger that you might fall asleep behind the wheel—which is what we're trying to avoid by your staying at the ranch in the first place."

She nodded and had to admit that he was making sense. "Okay, you win. Take me to your place."

He ushered her over to his Jeep. "I thought you'd never ask."

She wondered if it was her imagination, but his grin did look rather wicked.

# Chapter Seven

On second thought, it *wasn't* a wicked grin, it was just sleepy, wishful thinking on her part, Val decided, nothing more. If she wasn't so sleepy, she would have been able to hold the thought at bay—or maybe it wouldn't have even occurred to her in the first place.

She'd already told her mother, all of her friends and even herself a couple of times that she didn't want to venture into the turbulent waters of a relationship again yet—no matter how enticing the man in the center of those waters might be. For now, she was done with that.

Maybe forever.

Granted, she'd gotten married much too young and, who knew, had Scott lived they might have even been divorced by now—although she rather doubted it.

But she was smart enough to know that the man you love at eighteen is not always the one you still love at twenty-six; while Scott had a lot of adorable aspects to him, there had been some serious points of conflict between them that had only begun to emerge just before he'd died.

Still, her heart told her that they would have survived

all that and continued to be in love. Now she'd never know. All she did know was that she just wouldn't go through that pain of loss again.

"You look serious," Rafe commented, looking at the expression that had descended over her face as she got into the Jeep.

Val began to buckle up. She'd been smiling or on the verge of smiling all day and he'd gotten accustomed to seeing that smile on her face. Right now, she looked as if she was a million miles away, trying to figure out how to get back.

"Something wrong?" he asked. When she made no answer, he tried again. "Anything you want to share, or that I can do?" he prodded. Getting in, Rafe pulled his seat belt out and secured it.

"Hmm?" His voice had broken into her thoughts and she realized she'd gotten sidetracked again. Instantly, she flashed a wide, yet weary smile in his direction. There was no way she was about to tell him what she was thinking.

"No, this is my tired face," Val apologized. "You were right. Driving an extra fifty miles right now would *not* be a good idea, but I'm still a little concerned that your father is going to think I'm trying to take advantage of him by turning up like this."

"Not a problem," he assured her. "Trust me, there's nothing Dad likes better than being taken advantage of by a pretty girl." Rafe inserted his key into the ignition, turned it and let his Jeep warm up. "And you definitely qualify."

Val laughed softly, shaking her head. It wasn't that

she hadn't heard the words before, but coming out of his mouth, they somehow sounded nicer. She could even half believe that he meant them.

"You keep flattering me like that," she warned, "and you're going to wind up giving me a swelled head."

"I don't flatter, I call them as I see them," Rafe told her, trying to sound as serious as he could. "And from what I've seen today," he continued, being honest, "you seem pretty grounded to me. Grounded people don't get swelled heads."

"How would you know that I was grounded?" she questioned with a small, dismissive laugh. He'd only known her for—what?—twelve hours? Less?

"If you weren't grounded, you would have eaten up the attention you were getting at the diner. Eaten it up and played it up," he added.

"Have it your way," Val said with a surrendering sigh. "I'm too tired to argue the point." And she was. The rumbling engine was all but lulling her to sleep and she was fighting hard to keep her eyes opened. "Try me again tomorrow," she told him.

"Deal," he answered, then angled his head slightly in her direction as he backed out of his parking spot. He turned the vehicle around and headed for the outskirts of town and his family's ranch. "Hey, this okay?" he asked her.

The question seemed to come out of the blue. In addition, her eyelids began to feel as if each weighed just slightly less than a ton apiece.

"Is *what* okay?" she asked. As far as she could see,

nothing readily applied itself to the word *this* at the moment.

"The radio. I've got the station set to country, but if you'd rather listen to something else, I can switch stations for you," he offered.

"Country's fine," she told him, then added something that surprised him, since she came from the Southern-California coast. "I like country music."

He spared her a puzzled look. He would've expected her to favor some kind of popular, trendy music instead. "Really?"

"Uh-huh." Damn those eyelids, why were they so heavy and so impossible to hold up?

He wondered if she was pulling his leg. "Why?" Rafe pressed.

Her mind was drifting and she almost asked "why what?" before she remembered what the fledgling conversation was about. Country music. Something she'd recently gotten into.

"Because a lot of the songs tell a story. Makes me think," she answered in a low voice that turned into a whisper with the last word.

Just then, his engine made one of its odd noises, the way it did on occasion, and it managed to drown out the sound of her soft voice. He was about to ask Val to repeat what she'd just said when he saw that her eyes were now shut and her breathing had become very even.

Rafe smiled to himself knowingly. "Looks like the mighty location scout is pretty human after all," he mused aloud.

He turned his attention back to the darkened road

and continued to drive. Rafe absently wondered how long it would be before her scent faded from the interior of his vehicle.

Not soon, he hoped.

Reaching for the radio dial—the radio was as old as the vintage Jeep he drove—he lowered the volume a little just in case a loud song suddenly came on. He didn't want to chance waking her. He had a hunch she drove herself pretty hard and needed this rest.

An old, classic crying-in-your-beer song came on just as he straightened in his seat. The next moment, he became aware not of the words he heard but of the soft pressure against his shoulder. Val's head had fallen to the side and made contact with his shoulder. Fast asleep, she was using him as a pillow.

He supposed he could just gently push her back into her previous position, but again, he didn't want to wake her. And besides, he couldn't exactly say that he minded having her lean against him like this.

Without realizing it, he raised his foot off the accelerator just a little, slowing his speed from the acceptable fifty-five miles per hour down to forty.

After all, there was no real rush to get to the ranch now, was there?

ENTERING THE HOMESTRETCH and drawing close to the ranch house, Rafe was still debating what to do about the sleeping woman beside him. If he left her in the vehicle, she was bound to have a stiff neck when she finally did wake up in the morning. He didn't really feel right about waking her up, though.

He supposed he could just try to carry her inside, but he wasn't altogether certain how she'd react to that once she found out—or worse, if she woke up *while* he was carrying her. She might just assume that he was trying to get way too personal and take advantage of the situation as well as of her.

Rafe stopped the car.

They were here. No option presented itself ahead of the others.

"So what do I do here, Val?" he murmured under his breath, looking at her.

To his surprise, although he had kept his voice down when he'd voiced his dilemma aloud, he saw her eyelids flutter—and then her eyes slowly open.

He'd woken her up.

Val sighed, stretching. For a moment, there was a warm, sweet haze around her. And then her mind kicked in and she didn't recognize her surroundings.

Uttering a disoriented, startled, "Oh," she jerked her head up and straightened in the passenger seat. Only then did she realize that she'd had her head on Rafe's shoulder.

She flushed, at a loss as to whether to apologize or just pretend that she didn't realize that she'd been asleep. But a pretense like that felt vaguely dishonest, a label she knew people tended to want to slap onto "Hollywood types." She wasn't about to aid and abet that image if she could help it.

"I fell asleep," she murmured.

He couldn't help laughing softly. "Sure looked that way from where I was sitting."

She rotated her shoulders, working out the kinks. "Why didn't you wake me up?"

He did his best not to stare or get caught up in watching her stretch like that. "The whole point of driving you out here was to let you get some rest," he said. "Besides, having your head against my shoulder wasn't exactly an inconvenience."

She blinked and took a good look around. She recognized the building. "We're here," she realized. The last thing she remembered was being in the Jeep outside the diner. "How long was I asleep?" she asked, somewhat annoyed with her own lack of discipline.

"I think I got a chance to put the key into the ignition," he deadpanned.

Just as she thought. She'd slept the entire drive to the ranch. Some company she was, she thought ruefully. "Sorry about that."

He looked at her. "Why?"

Val laughed, shrugging her shoulders and feeling a tad self-conscious. It wasn't a familiar feeling for her. "Seemed like the thing to say. I guess you really were right about my not taking a chance and driving those fifty extra miles. I don't think I would have stayed awake even if I *was* driving."

"The open road has a way of being less than exciting and if you're tired, it's like taking a sleeping pill."

She had always had a habit of dropping off and then sleeping like a rock. To be honest, she was surprised that she had woken up when she had.

"What were you going to do if I hadn't woken up?" Val asked, curious.

Luckily, he didn't have to cross that bridge now. "Well, I was trying to decide what to do when you opened your eyes, so I guess we'll never know—unless you fall asleep again while I'm driving." And that didn't seem very likely, he speculated.

Unbuckling his seat belt, Rafe opened the door on his side, but instead of getting out, he paused to look at her and asked, "You ready to go in? Or do you want a couple of extra minutes?"

He'd meant that she might need more time to wake up, but Val obviously took his words to mean something else. She pulled down the sun visor on her side and looked into the mirror she'd noticed earlier. It turned out to be too dark to see.

"Why?" she asked him. "Do I look that bad?"

"Val, I don't think you could look bad if you tried," he told her matter-of-factly,

A wide smile spontaneously spread over her face. Despite its size, it still managed to be a tender, private smile.

"Rafe Rodriguez, you do say the nicest things," she told him.

Impulsively, she leaned over the transmission stick that separated them and brushed her lips against Rafe's cheek.

At least, his cheek was what she was aiming for. What she wound up making contact with at the last possible second, though, were his lips. And *that* happened because he'd turned his head to look at her again after she'd said what she had.

What began as a sweet, friendly gesture wound up turning into something more.

A great deal more.

It was difficult to say who was the more surprised of the two.

Or the more receptive.

Or who actually made the next move. The first move had been hers—the identity of the second move's initiator, the move that turned a sweet, innocent kiss into something a great deal more potent, was lost between them as each reacted to the accidental contact with a great degree of awe and suppressed passion.

Valentine's breath caught in her throat and her heart stood still for exactly a fraction of a second before both came back with a vengeance.

She knew that she should pull away, that she was still rather sleepy and thus a great deal more prone to being vulnerable and more open to what he had to offer.

If she hadn't just opened her eyes and come to, her guard wouldn't have been down. But it *was* down and it *was* breached. Swiftly and cleanly.

Her pulse raced and refused to settle down. Instead, it climbed ever higher as she sank into the delicious, arousing promise that was just beneath the surface of Rafe's kiss.

*Push him away! Push* yourself *away! Just do* something *to stop this before you can't. Before you reach that point of no return.*

That little voice in her head that always made such sense fairly screamed at her now and she knew, *knew* she should listen to it or she'd live to regret her rash action soon.

Extremely soon.

*Think, damn it, Val. Think! You can't do this. There are consequences...*

She had to work with these people, she couldn't just melt into one of them, no matter how tempting he was, or how much his mouth made her crazy. She couldn't let this happen.

Otherwise, if she did continue the way her freshly awakened inner core was begging her to, as a consequence "awkward" was going to hit new highs—or lows, depending on the interpretation.

She had to stop and she was going to stop—

In a second...

Any second now she'd pull her head back, murmur something witty or droll—anything but sigh—and this, as well as her about-to-break-the-sound-barrier pulse, would all be just pleasant history very, very soon.

Any second now...

And then, suddenly, she could feel air against her face—and there was space between her and Rafe. Space to slip more than just an envelope through.

Val blinked, trying very hard to get her bearings—and to wrap her head around what had just happened.

And why it had stopped happening.

Most of all, she waited for her wildly beating pulse to settle down to a normal rhythm.

"I'm sorry," Rafe said. His voice was low because he didn't quite trust it not to crack or squeak just yet.

Somehow his two words filled the entire interior of

the Jeep, growing so ominous they threatened to split the cab wide open.

"I don't know what came over me," Rafe confessed with an all-but-helpless shrug. "I didn't mean to force myself on you like that," he was saying. His eyes caressed her face. "It's just that you really make it so hard to just back away."

Val stared at him for a moment, making an effort to absorb the words coming out of his mouth. Holding them to her. Because from where she'd sat, she had started to think that it was all her, that she was the instigator, the one responsible for what had just transpired—and here he was, saying the exact same thing and apologizing for it.

Really? He thought *he* was the one behind that absolutely explosive kiss?

Well, maybe he was a little, she conceded, but there was no way on earth that the blame fell squarely and only on his shoulders. She wasn't some innocent bystander. She was as involved in this as he was.

Worst-case scenario, it was a shared responsibility. Because that sounded good to her, Val decided to go with that.

Touching his face, she said, "You didn't."

It was his turn to feel lost. He looked at her. "Didn't what?"

"Didn't force yourself on me," she clarified. "I'm a big girl now, Rafe, and I am very capable of fending off unwanted attention." She paused, taking a breath. "At the risk of being too honest—yours wasn't."

Had to be the intoxicating effect of her mouth. His

normally able, intelligent brain wasn't absorbing much. Whole sentences were sliding down the sides of his brain like so many slippery soap bubbles.

"Mine wasn't what?" he was forced to ask.

"Unwanted. Your attention wasn't unwanted," she told him softly just before she turned in the seat and swung her legs out of the passenger side of the Jeep.

There was no sense in leaving herself open to temptation any more than she already had, Val silently lectured herself.

"Let's go tell your dad about his unwanted house guest," she urged. She wanted to get into a house with lights and other people milling around before she suddenly decided to throw her arms around his neck and pull him to her again.

This was *not* the proper way to conduct business, she silently asserted.

"You're not," he told her as he walked a step behind her to the front door.

She turned to look at him. It was like being in an eternal tennis match except that rather than balls, they were lobbing comments at one another. Comments that seemed to hint at the people beneath them.

"Not what?"

"Unwanted," he answered.

She nodded after a moment, suddenly feeling as if she was living on borrowed time, biding her time until the inevitable finally happened.

And, unless she completely missed her guess, the "inevitable" that was going to happen to her involved Rafe.

## Chapter Eight

"You're absolutely *sure* that this is all right?" she asked as Rafe reached inside the dark room and turned on the light for her. The empty bedroom had some feminine touches throughout without being traditionally "girlie."

"I'm absolutely sure," he answered. "This used to be Alma's old room. Dad likes to keep things the way they were, just in case there's need for an overnight stay." He saw the skeptical look in her eyes and illustrated his point. "Last Christmas Eve, every room was filled. Dad likes having all of us over for dinner and then we all open our gifts at midnight—like we did when we were kids. Dad's very big on tradition."

"How is he on uninvited guests?" Val countered.

"Dunno," he replied honestly. "Because all our guests were always invited by someone and I invited you. End of debate." He could feel the strong, wiry feelings unfurling within him and all but reaching out to her. If he didn't walk away soon, he wasn't going to be able to. He didn't want her thinking he'd invited her for a little grab-and-feel session—no matter how tempting that notion might be. "See you in the morning," he told her and then very deliberately pulled himself away. "Good night."

"Good night," Val echoed.

As she closed the door she realized that she'd done a complete one-eighty. While her eyes had been too heavy to keep open earlier and she'd actually fallen asleep in his Jeep, now every single nerve ending she possessed was amped to its maximum level—and then some.

There was no way she was going to fall asleep soon, or easily, she told herself. The hour was late, but it was earlier back home in Los Angeles. Val decided to check in with her mother.

She had a great relationship with her mother. Despite the fact that the woman had a full-time career, Gloria Halladay wasn't one of those women who handed her child over to a housekeeper or a nanny and then pretended to listen to progress reports every so often. She was a very "hands on" mother. The trouble, if anything between them could be labeled "trouble," was that at times her mother forgot just how to take her "hands off."

But they were working on it, Val thought as she flopped on the bed and took out her cell phone. And, she smiled to herself, they really were making progress on that front.

Sort of.

She heard the phone on the other end being picked up after one incomplete ring. Which meant that her mother was all but sitting on her own cell phone. That, in turn, meant that her mother wasn't about to take her lack of communication yesterday in stride.

Val suppressed the desire to sigh. Instead, she cheerfully said, "Hello," the second the phone on the other end was picked up.

Her mother obviously recognized her voice and instantly pounced. "Ah, the prodigal daughter finally remembers her mother's cell phone number. I was beginning to get really concerned, Valentine."

Val braced herself. *Here it comes.*

"And I don't have to tell you that it was all I could do to keep your father from putting together some of his old buddies and forming a search party. He threatened to fly out to Texas with them and go looking for you. You know how he is."

*And I know how you are, too, Mom.*

Val closed her eyes. She could just *see* the scenario her mother was alluding to, she thought, embarrassment claiming both cheeks and marking them with a none-too-flattering pink hue. You could see the flush from outer space, but all she had to do was look in the mirror. The joys of being an only child meant that her parents were involved in her life big-time. She knew she should be grateful that they cared about her to this extent, but not for the first time, she wished there'd been a sibling so her parents could feel as if they had a spare in case something didn't pan out with their first born. Maybe then she would have had a little leeway to make a few mistakes and not feel as if the world might come to an end if she didn't call in on time.

Humoring the woman on the other end, the woman who she *did* love dearly, Val apologized. That, ultimately, was a lot better than arguing long distance, she told herself philosophically.

"I'm sorry I didn't call yesterday, but I got caught up in things."

"This 'thing' you got caught up in," her mother questioned, "does he have a name?"

Val rolled her eyes. She should have known it would go this way. It seemed that every other conversation she had with her mother these days seemed to revolve around the question: Did you meet anyone yet? Anyone was not just a vague reference to humanity in general but to a potential mate, specifically. It didn't matter that she'd already been married once, widowed once. All that mattered was that she was steadily approaching the age of thirty, never mind that she still had three years to go. What if those three years turn out to be as barren as the past few had been? Thirty was equated to being doomed to dying single, with an empty womb, according to her family, not medical certainty.

Her mother really was old-fashioned in certain ways, she couldn't help thinking.

"My job, Mom, I got caught up in my job," Val stressed. "I'm scouting a location for Jim Sinclair's new movie, remember?" It was a rhetorical question, seeing as how her mother had been the one who'd done the casting on this movie for Jim.

"I remember," Gloria said, dismissing that part of her daughter's protest. "I also remember that you always call to let us know you're all right, so when you didn't…"

Maybe if she drew up her own emancipation proclamation, put it in writing so that her mother had something to read before each phone call, they wouldn't have to waltz around the same basic issue every time.

"I love you to death, Mom, but I'm a big girl now, remember? Remember all those candles I blew out on my last birthday cake?" she stressed. "You don't have to worry about me anymore."

"Sorry, that's not what's in my contract," Gloria informed her daughter. "I get to worry about you for the first hundred years. After that, you're on your own, kiddo." And then her voice grew serious. "And besides, no matter how old you get or how many times you'll feel compelled to throw an ever-increasing number in my face, you will still always be my little girl and I will still always be thirty years older than you. That gives me seniority—and the right to worry. Your father feels the same way."

"Mom—" Val began, a definite warning note in her voice.

Gloria cut her off. "Oh, I can't wait for you to have kids of your own, Val. *Then* you'll understand this conversation from my side of it. *And* apologize for it."

"If you say so, Mom," Val said wearily. Her mother worried too much, there was no two ways about it.

"I say so. And I know so," Gloria said with conviction. Her voice grew just a little softer as she added, "I'd apologize to your grandmother for all the grief I gave her now that I see things from her seat, but unfortunately, she's not around."

This was something new. "You gave Grandma grief?" Val asked, immediately intrigued. "Care to unload any details?"

"That's not the part you're supposed to latch on to, kiddo," her mother chided. "And no, I'm not about to unload any details. But you might want to enlighten me as to where you are and why you haven't called me until now? Is everything all right?"

There was that concerned note again, Val thought, vacillating between feeling guilty and being annoyed. "Everything's fine. I am in Forever. Actually, I'm right outside Forever."

Gloria paused for a moment, as if trying to understand what her daughter had just said. "Is that a state of mind, Valentine? Are you becoming existential on me?"

"I'm being very straightforward with you, Mom," Val countered. "And 'Forever' isn't a state of mind, it's a town, a very small, tight little town located in Southern Texas. The people are nice and it is just *perfect* for Jim's movie."

There was another pause, as if her mother was dissecting what she'd just said and examining every word. "Uh-huh. What aren't you telling me?"

There were times when she was growing up that Val suspected her mother had a crystal ball which allowed her mother to monitor her 24/7 like some determined clairvoyant with tunnel vision. When she grew older, Val discarded that notion, laughing at the way she used to think.

But now she was beginning to believe that there was merit to her initial theory, at least to some degree. Her mother had honed in on her restless state, a state that had come into being because of a kiss that had no business exploding like that.

"What makes you think there's something I'm not telling you?" Val asked innocently. Perhaps a tad *too* innocently.

Her mother didn't utter the word "Aha!" but Val could feel it nonetheless. What the woman *did* say was, "Because I'm your mother and I know all your 'tells.'"

Now that was just plain silly. Her mother was just reaching. "You've got to be able to see a person to notice their 'tells,' Mom."

"Not necessarily," Gloria answered triumphantly. "There are the inflections in your voice, the pauses you make. You have your mysteries, dear, but you're also like a giant thousand-piece puzzle—one that comes with a cheat sheet. So again, what aren't you telling me?" Then, not waiting to be filled in, Gloria made a guess. Not for the first time. "You met someone."

"No! I mean, that is—" Tongue-tied, Val tried again. "Of course I met someone. I met people. I'm *always* meeting people. It's part of my job in scouting for the right location. But if you mean have I met an italicized *someone,* then the answer's no."

Her mother made a small, dismissive sound on the other end of the line, as if she knew better, then said, "Have it your way."

"Mom, I'm not 'having it my way,' I'm having it the way it was—*is,*" she stressed, then went on to business, which in this case also served as a lifeline for her. "What I do have to tell you is that the guy whose ranch we're going to be using if Jim approves—"

Gloria cut in with a very knowing, "He will."

"Please don't jinx it, Mom," she requested. "We don't know that for a fact yet."

"*You* might not, but I do," Gloria told her confidently. "I happen to know that Jim has great faith in you."

If her mother was going to keep interrupting, they would be on the phone until dawn. "Do you want to hear the rest of this or not?"

"Why, of course, dear," her mother said in that tone that always drove her crazy. "I always want to hear anything you want to say."

Val bit back another sigh. There were times that her mother played the magnanimous mother figure with a bit too much swagger. She supposed it came from having been around actors her entire life.

"What I wanted to tell you is that the guy whose house we'll be using is a big fan."

There was a shadow of confusion as Gloria asked, "Of Jim's?"

"No, Mom, of *yours*." It had been a while since her mother had been on the other side of the camera, but Val knew that her mother had treasured those years and, on occasion, missed being an actress.

"Of mine?" Gloria asked incredulously.

She could practically *see* her mother preening right over the phone. Once a budding actress, always a budding actress, Val thought, smiling to herself. That was what her father had affectionately told her mother when he saw her light up like the proverbial Christmas tree because someone had approached her for an autograph at their local grocery store a few months ago. She'd signed the man's shirt with a flourish—he had no paper available—and then posed for a photograph.

"Of course, of yours," Val told her. "Said he always wondered why you stopped making movies."

"Because I had a real, live production of my own to take care of," she heard her mother say. Her mother never tired of phrasing it that way, Val couldn't help thinking. "What's this man's name? Maybe I'll send him an autographed picture. I'm assuming you'll take care of supplying me with an address."

"No problem, Mom. Coincidentally, I'm staying at his ranch right now." The moment the words were out of her mouth, she *knew* she was going to regret them.

Sure enough, regret began immediately as her mother said, "Oh? And just how old is this man who's pretending to be a fan?"

"He's not pretending," Val said, feeling protective of Rafe's father. "And he's about Dad's age." She knew that her parents were only one year apart, but she never equated anyone to her mother's age since the working theory was that Gloria Halladay was ageless.

Or at least liked to think of herself in those terms.

In reality, her mother *did* look a lot younger than her age. Val could only hope that sort of thing had been passed on to her via her mother's genes.

Instantly, the lioness intent on guarding her cubs was back. "Valentine, I'd feel better if you stayed at a hotel."

"Would if I could, Mom," Val informed her mother cheerfully, "but they don't have a hotel in this town."

"No hotel?" Gloria asked, horrified. Hotels were the

last bastion of civilization to her. "Where *are* you, the last ring of hell?"

Val strove for patience. "I already told you where I am, Mom. The town is called Forever and it's really a very nice place. It just hasn't gotten around to building a hotel, that's all."

"Call Jim the second you hang up," her mother instructed, tackling the situation in her usual no-nonsense way. "Once he okays the location, maybe I can persuade him to send out one of those large trailers for you—"

Val closed her eyes. "I'm fine, Mom," she said wearily.

She apparently was *not* convincing her mother. "But what if he—?"

Val cut her off. "He won't. Besides, he's got three of his sons still living on the ranch. Think of them as chaperones."

"Three sons?" There was renewed interest in her mother's voice. The protective lioness had retreated into the wild.

*And she's back,* Val couldn't help thinking. "Down, Mom, I'm not on an episode of *The Bachelorette.* I'm just doing my job," she emphasized.

Gloria was trying another approach to the same end goal. "All work and no play makes Jane—"

"A very rich girl," Val interjected. "Oops, gotta go, Mom, I hear another call coming in. Must be Jim. Love to Dad."

"But—"

Before her mother could say anything else in protest, Val terminated the call. There wasn't another one coming in, but she was getting sleepy again and she just wasn't equipped for a battle of wits with someone like her mother, a woman she was fairly certain *never* slept.

The moment she disconnected her mother, her phone vibrated again. Val sighed. The sigh went all the way down to her toes. Her mother was nothing if not persistent. Maybe next Christmas she'd rent some grandchildren for the woman to play with, she thought in frustration.

Pressing the "accept" button, Val sought to cut her mother off at the very beginning. "Look, Mom, I haven't got any more time to talk to you now. I've got to call Jim."

"Glad to hear that," the deep male voice said into her ear. "I guess that means I'm saving you the trouble of pressing all those pesky buttons in order to make that call."

The voice she heard was a complete contrast to the one she was expecting to hear. It took her a second to reorient herself. "Jim?"

"Good, you still remember the sound of my voice. I was beginning to worry, not to mention give up hope."

As if anyone could forget the deep, rumbly voice, she thought. "Well, your hope is about to be restored, Jim. I have found *the* perfect place for the movie. The perfect ranch, the perfect town," she enthused.

"Go on," the director encouraged.

"I've got a better idea," she told him. "Rather than my going on and describing the place to you, why don't you just take a look at the pictures I've been taking? I'll send them to your phone," she offered. "Trust me, this place looks *exactly* like what you had in mind."

"Don't lead me on, Valentine," Jim warned. "I'm exceedingly vulnerable right now. There are rumors that the studio's firing Vance Steele and putting a real fire-breather in his place to head the studio. Lewis Daniels. The man has a reputation that makes Lucifer look good. No project is safe."

She knew the man he was referring to. Knew, too, that the man was firm, but fair. He just couldn't be talked out of anything once he'd made up his mind.

"The king is dead, long live the king," she murmured. It seemed to her like that was an ongoing thing. Every time a studio lost money or just broke even on a film rather than the piles of revenue it was anticipating, heads began to roll and people quaked in their shoes. Scapegoats were always in season.

It was, admittedly, a brutal business, but she still loved it.

The next moment, Jim complained, "I'm still looking at a screen full of nothing."

"Sorry, here comes something," she told him as she pressed the right combination of keys to make the transfer happen. When there was nothing but silence on the other end, she grew uneasy. Had she misjudged exactly what he was looking for?

"Well?" she pressed.

"You're teasing me, right?" Jim accused. "You haven't come up with anything and this is your way of having fun."

He'd completely lost her. Maybe she should have had

this call go to voice mail and just gone to bed the way any sane, normal person would have. "What are you talking about, Jim?"

"This is too perfect," he answered. "Every photo you just sent looks just like the sketches I had Sylvia make up at the outset," he said, referring to the woman who had set up the movie's storyboard.

"I just sent you some of the photos I've been taking around the area. This place exists," she argued. "I knew it was perfect the second I saw it. Now all I need to know is if *you* like it."

"Like it?" he echoed incredulously. "If this place had hands, I'd slip an engagement ring on the appropriate finger. I *love* it," he declared with feeling. "Start the negotiations."

He caught her off guard with his last instruction. "I thought that you'd send Henderson to do that."

"Henderson's down with the flu and I want this place as soon as possible. I want it yesterday. Promise them anything it takes—up to the limit."

"And if the limit isn't enough?" she asked, even though she was fairly sure that Miguel would accept the offer with no argument. The amount of money involved had already left him close to speechless when she'd first mentioned it.

"Raise the limit," he told her without hesitation. "I want that location." He made it clear that failure to secure it was not an option. "Call me the minute you seal the deal. I'll have the crew out within two days. And, Valentine—"

She was about to terminate the call, but stopped when he said her name. "Yes?"

"I'm counting on you. Make this happen."

"You got it."

*No pressure here,* she thought cryptically as she finally ended the call. Not that she thought Rafe's father would turn her down. He all but came out and said yes to her. It was just that she didn't like taking anything for granted. Because when you took something for granted, that was when the gods decided to pull the rug right out from under your feet and you wound up hitting your head and being rushed off to the hospital.

Or, in her specific case, she'd believed that she was going to be married until she was old and gray—and possibly longer. And then, suddenly, rather than looking forward to celebrating anniversaries and having children, there she was, holding a wake for Scott and trying desperately to hold herself together.

Putting her phone away, she shut off the light, then lay back in bed and closed her eyes, willing herself to wind down again. She needed her sleep. Come morning, she had people to see and deals to finalize.

## Chapter Nine

Ordinarily, she could sleep anywhere, any time. Her father liked to joke that she could probably sleep hanging in the closet on a wire coat hanger. But tonight, sleep took its own sweet time in coming to her.

Val didn't know exactly when she finally did manage to drift off, but it had taken her quite a while—and then there was dawn, slipping in through the open curtains, making itself known as it nudged her awake.

Feeling like something that the cat had dragged in, Val stared at the ceiling for a couple of moments, trying to orient herself and remember exactly where she was. Waking up in beds that weren't her own wasn't unusual for her. Because of the nature of her job, she traveled a great deal. Even so, putting a name to her latest locations was tricky for her at times.

Like now.

And then she remembered.

Remembered discovering the ranch and feeling confident that she had lucked out. Remembered Jim's pleased voice when she'd sent the photographs she'd taken of the ranch. Remembered feeling good because she'd been right.

Remembered Rafe's kiss.

The last had her smiling languidly for exactly ten seconds, and then she bolted upright when her thoughts began to take her to places she had absolutely no business going.

Places that, while wonderful, she'd already been to and had no intention of revisiting. Because those places were coupled with disappointment and heartache. She knew that as certainly as she knew that night followed day.

Enough of this "castles in the sky" nonsense. She needed to get going, Val told herself. Grabbing her discarded shirt, jeans and boots, she rushed into the bathroom, hoping that a quick shower would make a new person out of her—or at the very least, revive the person she'd been before moonlight and Rafe had robbed her of her ability to focus clearly.

Fifteen minutes later, Val was sailing down the stairs, ready to do whatever it took to get Miguel Rodriguez to agree to lease the production company the use of his ranch for their movie.

Preoccupied, she sailed right into Rafe, who was just about to go upstairs to knock on her door and wake her.

Obviously, he thought wryly, that was unnecessary at this point.

Catching hold of Val's shoulders to keep from knocking her down, he was surprised at how sturdy they felt. This was not some delicate little flower no matter *what* she looked like.

"Whoa. Where are you going in such an all-fired hurry?" he asked. When she looked first at one of her shoulders, then the other before fixing him with a stare, he dropped his hands from them and held them up as if in partial surrender.

"The kitchen," she answered, banking down a wave of embarrassment because she'd almost run him down. "I wanted to catch your father at breakfast."

"He's still very 'catchable,'" Rafe assured her. "Trust me, right now, he's not going anywhere." Captivated, he cocked his head as if to study her a little more closely. He could see that she really didn't look all that rested. "You sleep well?"

He'd called it, she thought. For the most part, she believed in telling things the way they were. But, seeing as how what had kept her up were the after-effects of his kiss, that really wasn't something she wanted to share with him right now.

Most likely, never.

She wanted to focus on presenting her most charming, convincing side—to him as well as to his father and the rest of his family. Jim was eager to get started shooting and he was sold on this place. There was a lot riding on her powers of persuasion, not the least of which was giving her an excuse to be in Forever and around Rafe without appearing to be going out of her way.

If she was being honest with herself right now, she wasn't sure what it was that she was looking for at this point in her life. She'd been in love, been a wife and been a widow. And while she missed the emotions associated with the first two, she did *not* miss the pain that came with the third.

She supposed that the best that she could hope for right now was that, with any luck, she'd recognize what she was looking for when she finally saw it.

"Slept like a log," she answered cheerfully.

Rafe's eyes narrowed ever so slightly as they washed over her again, this time ever so slowly. "A log that was being taken downriver by enterprising loggers after they'd just cut it down," he judged. Then, before she could protest his assessment, he told her what he knew she'd want to hear. "By the way, he said yes."

The words, coming out of the blue like that, stunned her. "Who said yes?"

"My dad," he answered simply, then, because she was still looking at him uncertainly, he added, "He said yes to having your crew out here, filming in the area and using our ranch."

"You made my pitch for me?" Why would he do that? Especially without telling her?

He shrugged like it was no big deal. "I'm a good listener," he told her. "I just repeated what you'd said yesterday. Figured you wouldn't start out by offering to pay less for the use of the ranch than you did the day before. Since he already seemed sold on you yesterday, I figured this was already a done deal, and I was right. There was no need to negotiate." Rafe smiled at her. "Now you can relax and have your breakfast without trying to work it past the knot in your stomach."

The way he seemed to see right through her was a little unnerving. "What makes you think that there's a knot in my stomach?" she asked. Val had always prided herself on how relaxed and friendly she came across. Using only a handful of words, Rafe had totally negated that self-image.

"Because I knew you wanted to do a good job," he explained, "and everyone who's worth their salt always worries about things going south on them—which means they've got knots in their stomach. Nothing to be ashamed of," he told her.

"Like an actor having stage fright before they go on," she countered.

Rafe inclined his head after a beat, unable to relate to the image she'd just described. But he was fairly confident that it carried significance for her and underscored what he'd just said. He felt it was fairly safe to agree.

"Yeah, like that," he said with as much conviction as he could summon for a metaphor that meant utterly nothing to him.

"Is your dad in the kitchen?" she asked. "I'd like to thank him."

"Yeah, he's just finishing up his breakfast. Mike and Ray have already had breakfast and left," he added.

Just as well, she thought. She'd gotten the feeling that the oldest son didn't approve of filming on the family ranch and she would really rather talk to the senior Rodriguez without having to incur any negative vibes from a member of his family.

Val hurried past Rafe, wanting to see the older man while his acceptance was still fresh.

"Good morning," she said brightly, reaching the kitchen and walking into the bright, sun-splashed room with its burnt orange tiled floor, rimmed in blue. Had anyone mentioned the melding of these two colors to her, she would have cringed at least inwardly if not outright. But seeing them now side by side, they actually worked, she thought, glancing down at the floor.

The bright, glazed colors made the room seem larger and welcoming—as if the presence of the older Rodriguez with his bright, warm smile wasn't already welcoming enough.

Ever the courtly gentleman, Miguel half rose in his chair. "Good morning, Valentine. I take it you slept well?"

"The fresh air works miracles," she said, hoping he would accept that as her affirmative answer without her having to actually fudge the truth. The sympathetic smile she received in response made her realize that Miguel Sr. was reading between the lines and had gotten the true answer to his question. He seemed to know not only that she'd had a restless night, but why—in general—it had been a restless night for her.

Like father, like son, she thought again, getting a definite feeling of déjà vu. If she had the opportunity to play poker with either of these two men, she wouldn't, she decided.

"Take a seat," Miguel said, gesturing toward the place setting that had been reserved for her.

Nodding her thanks, Val sat down, noting with a measure of relief that Rafe was staying, as well. He took the seat beside her as his father sat down again, facing them.

There were covered dishes in the center of the table.

He'd done that, she knew, to keep whatever he was offering warm for her. The man took his hospitality very seriously.

"We still have some breakfast left," Miguel was saying, "although these boys of mine, especially Ramon and Miguel, they eat like locusts, like tomorrow there will be a famine," he explained. "I had to remind them that we had a guest staying with us."

Acutely aware that she had imposed on his hospitality without having actually received an invitation from him, she took this opportunity to make her apologies. "About that, Mr. Rodriguez, I hope that you don't mind—"

"Mind?" he echoed, interrupting her because he wanted to spare her any discomfort. "Why should I mind having such a lovely person grace us with her presence? It has been a long time since Alma lived here," he confided with a twinge of wistfulness in his voice. "Once my daughter became the sheriff's deputy, she moved into town to be close to her work. And then, of course, she got married so now I only see her on the bigger occasions—"

"Like Sundays," Rafe pretended to whisper to her as an aside.

"Sundays are special," Miguel told his son. "Especially when everyone can come to dinner. But I usually get excuses instead of my children," he confided with a sigh. "But I understand. They have lives and are too busy to come by." Miguel milked the moment for sympathy. "It is the life of a parent to do everything he can to raise his children well—so that he can never see them except once in a while."

Rafe laughed. "This is where the violins come in," he told her.

"Violins? Why would violins come in?" Miguel asked. "Who would be playing these violins?"

Rafe shook his head. Maybe he'd hurt the old man's feelings. "That was just a joke, Dad."

"Tell a funny one next time," the older man instructed his son.

He turned his attention back to the young woman at his table. The one he had already decided would be a good match for this particular son. He could tell that they balanced one another out nicely. Now it was up to him to do whatever he could to make sure that the two would come together and realize what he already saw: That they would be good together—and that they would have beautiful babies.

"So, my dear," Miguel began, warming to his subject, "my son tells me that we will be seeing a great deal of you for the next two months or so."

She spared Rafe a glance. The latter raised his shoulders in a hapless gesture, silently telling her that he had said no such thing.

If that had truly been the case, that meant that there'd been more reading between the lines, Val thought. It made her feel somewhat defenseless if this knack of his was even partially operational.

"Well, I don't know about a great deal," she answered, trying to hedge slightly, "but I'll be here for a while during filming. And on that subject, thank you for agreeing that we can use your ranch house."

"My pleasure entirely," Miguel responded with another warm smile.

"And the check you'll be getting for letting them use the house doesn't hurt either. Right, Dad?" Rafe teased him.

Rather than deny it, Miguel nodded. "Money is always useful. It takes headaches away and if the bills are paid, it allows a man to focus on the more important things in his life. His family." Leaning forward over the table ever so slightly, he told Val, "I have endured worrying that the bills would not be paid and *this* is a far better way to approach life," he assured his guest. "Believe me."

Miguel was making this very easy for her and she wanted to reward him for that.

"I could perhaps negotiate a little more money for you," she told Rafe's father. "If you found the amount we initially talked about a little on the low side, then perhaps I could—"

Miguel raised his hand to stop her. "The amount is fine, Valentine," he assured her jovially. "But thank you for offering. I am a man of simple tastes and I do not wish to look as if I am being greedy, asking for more after you have already quoted such a generous amount to me."

Still, she wanted to do more. Something about the man compelled her to be generous. It wasn't her father complex kicking in. She loved her own father dearly and he was always there for her.

But Miguel Rodriguez was like a warm, huggable teddy bear of an uncle she wanted to do right by. "I also want you to know that if anything is damaged—not that it will be," she quickly assured him, afraid he might have second thoughts on the matter, "but if by some chance something *does* go wrong, we will pay for any and all repairs—or a replacement if that becomes necessary."

Miguel nodded, attempting to maintain a solemn expression on his face because he knew this was important for her.

"That is good to know. Now, eat," he instructed, gesturing toward the covered serving plates. "We cannot send you back to your mother looking as if we were trying to starve you."

Val was tempted to say that her mother hadn't had anything to say about how she chose to eat in a very long time, but she had a feeling that her consumption of food wasn't really the subject here.

Her mother was.

And then she thought of the perfect way to show her thanks to the senior Rodriguez for being so cooperative and nice.

Val measured out her words, watching his expression as she spoke. "You know, Mr. Rodriguez, my mother told me that she might come out here if she has a chance."

Instantly, Miguel's eyes gleamed in anticipation. "Your mother would come *here?*" he asked incredulously. "To Forever?"

Val nodded. "Well, she is the casting director for this film and sometimes she likes to watch a couple of days of filming to see if her casting instincts were right or if perhaps someone else might have filled a particular role better."

"I am sure her 'casting instincts' are perfect," Miguel replied. "Just as she is."

*Mother is going to absolutely love you,* Val thought. She saw Rafe's father look around his surroundings as if seeing them for the first time—or through different eyes. Eyes, undoubtedly, that belonged to the woman he had idolized for decades now.

"If your mother is to come here, then I will have to do some redecorating. It has been a long time since some of this furniture has been here," he recalled, frowning as he stared at a piece.

Maybe she'd gone a bit too far, Val thought. "Please don't change anything on my mother's account. She has very simple taste," she told Miguel. "I'm sure she'd find your home charming."

The expression on Miguel's face told her that he had his doubts. But for now, he would take her words under advisement. She could tell by his wide smile.

"LET ME APOLOGIZE for my father," Rafe said once breakfast was over and they were finally outside the house. "I'm afraid that he tends to get a little intense at times."

"No need to apologize," she assured Rafe. "I think he was adorable." She grinned. "And I completely understand that sudden attack of nerves that he was having back there."

"When?" As far as he could see, his father was just being a little too intense, but he was fairly accustomed to that. Being intense was all part of his father's more volatile side. It emerged whenever he became passionate, about a cause, or, in this case, a person. A person, he now realized, his father had fantasized about for years. The perfect woman he'd once overheard his father call her. At the time, he was just a teenager and he'd had no idea who Gloria Halladay was.

"At the end," she confided, "when he started talking about redecorating the whole house for my mother. That was a giant case of nerves," she pointed out. "Your father's starstruck and I get that—but my mother is just a very simple person."

The look he gave her reeked of disbelief. "Yeah, right."

"She is," Val insisted. "My mother was the one who made sure that I was well grounded, that my head wasn't turned by the over-the-top lifestyle of some of the kids I went to school with. She always cherished the simpler things in life, things money couldn't buy. She really is an old-fashioned girl at heart," she told Rafe.

Whether or not her mother was such a sterling person he had no idea, but he could tell that Val really believed she was.

"And are you?" he asked. "An old-fashioned girl at heart?" he added in case she misunderstood.

Val couldn't help the grin that came to her lips and she didn't bother to hide it. "Oh, you have no idea," she guaranteed.

He liked the look in her eye when she said it. Anticipation welled up within him, whispering promises in his ear.

## Chapter Ten

"See, there it is, safe and sound and none the worse for having spent a night out here, away from you," Rafe pointed out cheerfully as they drove up to the front of the diner. The slightly dusty powder-blue CRV was parked exactly where she had left it. "I told you that you had nothing to worry about."

"I didn't initially refuse your offer because I was worried something would happen to my car," she told him as he parked right beside her CRV. Val got out of the Jeep and rounded the rear of the vehicle. "I'm just used to doing things on my own."

"Nothing wrong with that," Rafe allowed. "Unless, of course, you get so stubborn that common sense goes out the window." He saw her open her mouth to protest, but he beat her to the punch. "Fortunately, you're not like that." Rafe shoved his hands into his pockets and rocked slightly on his heels. "So now what? You drive off into the sunset until the movie people come out, or—"

"Or." She picked the second option. "No point in wasting time going back and forth. Everything that I need to access I can get via either my smart phone or my netbook."

"Netbook?" Rafe echoed, raising one eyebrow as he looked at her. He'd heard of the former, but "netbook" was a new term for him.

"Think of it as a shrunken laptop." She patted the shoulder bag that was all but a part of her anatomy. Inside she carried around what she considered were all the electronic essentials of life—along with at least one set of backup batteries. For his benefit, she pulled out the eleven-inch netbook she had come to depend very heavily on. "These days, the smaller they are, the more powerful."

Rafe didn't look at the netbook she was holding up. Instead, his eyes washed over her at the same time that amusement entered them. "That's the feeling I get," he replied.

Their eyes locked for a moment, until Val glanced away. If she hadn't, she was positive that her cheeks would betray her and turn pink—and she absolutely hated when they did that. If nothing else, it went against the image she had of herself. She was supposed to be unflappable. Unflappable people *didn't* blush.

Changing the topic, she nodded at the diner. It was a little after eight in the morning. "Think Miss Joan is in yet?"

He laughed and Val looked at him quizzically. "Miss Joan is *always* in."

"I thought, being the owner, she'd have people working the morning shift for her so she could sleep in." Wasn't that the reward for a life of hard work? To get to the place where you were actually free to sleep in? "Doesn't she have a family?"

"Yeah, she does. You're looking at them," he told her, gesturing around the general area. "Miss Joan did get married not all that long ago, but her husband, Harry, understands that running the diner, being there to oversee everything's running smoothly, is what makes her happy. And Harry wants his wife to be happy.

"I guess you could say that Miss Joan's pretty much the town's lifeblood. That's part of the reason Harry loves her."

Because her whole life was centered around making and watching movies, as Val listened to Rafe tell her about Miss Joan, she felt that there was a story in here somewhere and for her, all stories just naturally turned into movies in her head.

She headed toward the diner's front steps. Val learned a long time ago never to take anything—or anyone— for granted. "Well, then I'd better tell the town's 'lifeblood' that Jim was thrilled with the photographs of the town that I sent."

Rafe was right behind her. "Jim?"

Val paused for a moment to fill him in. Jim Sinclair was so much a part of her life that there were times she forgot not everyone knew the man. "Jim Sinclair, the director of the movie."

She took the three steps to the diner's door quickly and walked in.

Miss Joan was behind the counter, talking to a tall, dark-haired man in a uniform seated in front of her. He was nursing a cup of steaming black coffee. When the owner of the diner raised her eyes to watch her approach, the man seated at the counter turned on the stool to see who had come in. Val saw a star pinned to his shirt. This had to be the law in Forever.

Taking a last sip of his coffee, the man nodded at Rafe. "Rafe."

"'Morning Miss Joan, Sheriff." Rafe greeted the duo in the order he deemed most appropriate, then turned toward Val. "Rick, this is—"

"Valentine Jones," Sheriff Rick Santiago completed with a nod toward the woman with Rafe. "Yes, I know. Miss Joan already filled me in." He smiled at Val. "So you're the one bringing the movie crew to our town."

That gave her way too much credit, Val thought. She never presented herself to be more important in the scheme of things than she was. "I'm just the one making recommendations. The final decision lies with my boss." She looked from Miss Joan to the sheriff. "But for the record, my boss thinks that your town is just perfect."

"Most of us here think so," the sheriff told her.

Val's eyes shifted toward the woman she had come in to see. "I wanted to tell you that it's official. I sent the photos I took of the town and the Rodriguez ranch to my boss and he agrees with me. Forever is just the way he envisioned the location for his film would look. Filming starts as soon as they can get everyone out here."

Miss Joan nodded. "Appreciate you giving me the head's up. And just so *you* know," she went on, "the town council had their meeting here last night and the vote went in your favor. Just keep it orderly," the woman added, sounding like a teacher about to let her class out for recess in the schoolyard.

"It's a good group of people coming out," Val assured her. "There won't be any rowdy incidents. Jim, the director, likes to use the same crew on all his pictures. This way, they know what he means when he says something and they're familiar with his style. It's more efficient that way and it makes for faster filming," she explained. "He'll be bringing the contracts with him to sign. With the money the town will be getting, you can afford to build an official place where you can hold your meetings."

"Nothing wrong with having the meetings in here," Miss Joan told her, then shrugged. "But we'll see. Always good to have money on hand for emergencies," she added.

Relieved that she hadn't somehow managed to insult the woman, Val nodded. "Oh, and one last thing." She'd mentioned this the day before. "There is going to be a need for extras on the film," she reminded the woman. "So anyone who's ever fancied seeing himself or herself on the screen, this is their chance to make that happen."

"We can post that on the bulletin board," Miss Joan told her, nodding toward the rectangular corkboard that was mounted by the door. A few notices were currently pinned to the surface. "Most everyone in Forever comes here for a meal or their morning coffee or *something* so if anyone's interested in smiling for the camera, they'll see the notice."

"Actually, they'd have to act like they don't see the

camera. That's the whole point," Val explained. "Extras provide the human background in a movie."

Miss Joan nodded. "Why don't you put all that down and we'll post it?" she suggested. Turning her head, she called out, "Rayleen, why don't you go into my office and bring out a sheet of paper and a pen for me?"

"Right away, Miss Joan," one of the waitresses immediately replied, hurrying off to the back.

"She'll be just a minute," Miss Joan promised. Glancing to her left, she saw someone taking a seat at the far end of the counter. "Excuse me for a minute," she said just before making her way to the new arrival.

"Time to get to work," Rick said to no one in particular as he got off his stool. Taking out a bill, he left it on the counter beside his cup. "I need to leave before Miss Joan gets back," he told Val. Tipping the brim of his hat to her, he added, "Nice meeting you."

That was odd, she thought as the sheriff made his way out of the diner. She turned to look at Rafe. "Why does he have to go before she gets back?"

Rafe laughed. "Because Miss Joan insists that the coffee is on the house while the sheriff tells her that he doesn't want to take advantage of the badge. It's an ongoing thing, my sister tells me. Both of them are stubborn as hell in their own way," he confided.

Someone always had to be more so, Val thought. "My money's on Miss Joan," she said.

She expected Rafe to agree with her since he was the one who'd told her that the woman always got her way but he surprised her. "Mine's on Rick. According to Alma and Gabe, the sheriff can be *really* stubborn when he wants to be."

At that point, Miss Joan returned. Looking at the counter, she frowned at the money left beside the empty coffee cup.

"That man," she murmured in exasperation. Taking out a jar from beneath the counter, she set it down beside the cup and put the bill Rick had left through the slot on the top. "It's my charity jar," she explained to Val. "Anyone comes through here who's down on their luck, I give 'em whatever's been collected to help get them back on their feet."

Rafe smiled at the woman. "You give them much more than that."

Miss Joan snorted. "Nobody needs you running off at the mouth like that, boy. You're boring your lady friend here."

"I'm not bored at all," Val told the woman. "You know, the director likes to incorporate a little improvisation in the movies he makes." She grinned at the woman. "A savvy, sassy diner owner might be the very thing that will spark his imagination."

Miss Joan snorted dismissively, but Val had a really strong feeling that the woman wasn't nearly as indifferent as she pretended.

"Can I get you two something?" the woman asked, looking from Val to Rafe.

"No, thank you, nothing right now," Val replied. "I had a very large breakfast." Miguel wouldn't think of letting her leave until she'd had a little of everything the newly returned housekeeper had prepared. "Rafe's father made sure I was filled up to the gills."

Small, amber eyes took full measure of her. "That probably took all of two eyedroppers," Miss Joan theorized.

"Here's the pen and paper you asked for," the tall, slender dark-haired waitress Miss Joan had sent off to her office announced, putting both down on the counter.

Miss Joan in turn pushed the pen and paper toward Val. "Put down whatever you want the good citizens of Forever to know, then tack it up on that board," she instructed, nodding at the bulletin board she'd previously mentioned. Just as she nodded, two more people entered. The diner was starting to fill up.

Val began to write and Miss Joan said, "Well, thanks for the official heads-up. I'll see you around." With that, she went to wait on the two men who had just come in.

Val finished writing her notice. After reading it over, she decided it was good enough to tack up. "I guess Miss Joan'll take care of making sure that everyone reads this." There was no doubt in Rafe's mind that the woman would. Having a movie company in town, filming, was something that had never happened in Forever before. That made it a big deal.

"Count on it."

That was good enough for her, Val thought. Pausing by the door, Val took two of the thumbtacks that were stuck in on the side of the board and used them to tack up her sign. She placed it right in the middle. Satisfied, she left the diner. Rafe followed her down the steps.

She turned to look at him once she'd stepped to the

side of the steps. "Rafe, I would like to buy you the biggest, juiciest steak in town—my way of saying thanks for all your help."

"Well, not that I actually did anything—other than get you out of the bull's path yesterday," he amended. But that had been sheer instinct. Saving her from the bull had nothing to do with helping her with the scouting job she was on. "But I could always eat a good steak."

"The biggest, juiciest steak in town," she repeated. When Rafe laughed, Val stared at him. She couldn't understand why that was particularly funny to him. He'd just said he liked steak. "Why are you laughing?" she asked.

"Because Miss Joan's diner is the *only* place to eat in town so the 'biggest steak in town' would be right here, as well."

"No other little out-of-the-way cafés around here?" she asked. They hadn't gone on a full tour of the town yesterday and she knew that the diner was the main gathering place, but she just couldn't conceive of there being no other place to go.

"Nope."

She glanced over her shoulder at the diner. "Miss Joan has a monopoly, I take it."

He leaned against the hood of his vehicle, facing her. He supposed this was all very small time to a woman like her. "I guess you could see it that way. The rest of us just see it as the way things've always been. Cozy," he emphasized. "There is a saloon in town," he told her, "but the owner and Miss Joan have a deal going.

She doesn't serve hard liquor and they don't serve food. Everybody's happy."

He watched as her eyes lit up. Obviously, he'd said the right thing. "A real saloon? Or just another bar?"

The former suggested a place with character where interesting people turned up. The latter word made her think of a crammed little place where the lighting was dim and the people who frequented it were even dimmer.

"No, it's a saloon," he assured her. "Actually, it was here before Miss Joan came with her diner, at least that's what they tell me. I wouldn't know firsthand. Before my time," he explained.

She thought for a moment. "I don't remember seeing a saloon yesterday."

"That's because I didn't think you'd find it more interesting than the countryside or the reservation. Only so much a person can take in in one day," he said.

"Fair enough," she replied with a nod. "Take me there now," she said suddenly.

"You *want* to see the saloon?" he asked, somewhat surprised. She didn't strike him as someone who would want to set foot in a dark and rather boring place like that.

Val nodded. "Yes. I want to check it out. It might add some extra color to the movie."

Since the saloon had been part of the town for as long as he could remember, he didn't think about the place one way or another. Like Miss Joan's diner, it'd always been there, mainly for men looking to unwind and kick back a little. It had its place in Forever, but in his opinion, didn't play as much of a role in the town's day-to-day life as the diner did.

"I don't think people think of 'color' when they think of Jack's," he told her.

"What do they think of when they think of Jack's?" she asked, curious. She was always open to input. She'd discovered on her very first assignment, searching for the right location to film *The Twelfth Princess,* coincidentally another romantic comedy directed by Jim Sinclair, that you just never knew when you could pick up something to pass on, something useful to the production company.

Rafe grinned at her. "Something tall and cold and wet," he told her.

"In other words, a drink." More to the point, she thought, a tall glass of beer.

"Either that," Rafe deadpanned, "or a bartender who's been rained on."

"Very funny," she countered. "What time does the saloon open?"

She probably had to wait a few hours, she judged. It wasn't even close to noon yet. But she did want to explore the premises, see if it could fit into the framework of the story somehow. Half the movies she'd worked on with Sinclair were two-thirds scripted, one-third improvised. The latter was influenced by what the director saw once he got to the chosen location. He'd taught her that spontaneity was an integral part of any film.

"What time is it now?" Rafe asked in response to her question.

Her eyes widened. "You mean it's open this early?"

Why would a place that only serves alcohol be open at this hour? From what she'd seen of the town so far, its citizens didn't strike her as the type who needed to drown their sorrows on such an extreme basis that they began before the day was even underway.

He nodded. "The owners live above it and close the saloon down when the last customer goes home—or on the really rare occasion when all three of them feel too tired to continue serving drinks."

"So all three of them are co-owners?" Val asked him. "Do they take equal turns working behind the bar?"

He nodded. "They do, but it's pretty clear to everyone that it's Brett who really runs things. Most of the time, Liam and Finn just go along with whatever he says. Although," Rafe qualified as they walked, "lately Liam—that's the middle brother—has been acting as if he's getting kind of itchy."

"Itchy?" she echoed, slanting a quizzical look in Rafe's direction.

"Yeah, itchy," he repeated with emphasis. "You know, like he wants to leave Forever. Get out and see what the world has to offer. Itchy," he repeated with emphasis this time.

"I see. How does Brett react to this 'itchiness'?" she asked, trying to absorb the family dynamics of the establishment she was going to see.

Rafe shrugged. "He pretends it's not happening. I think he figures it's a stage that Liam's going through and it'll fade away eventually."

"And Finn?"

He laughed. "When he's not working there, Finn's too busy chasing girls to notice anything."

"Sounds like an average red-blooded boy," she commented with a smile. Then, giving him a long glance as they walked to Jack's, she asked, "Do you ever get 'itchy?'"

Rafe looked at her as if the question made no sense to him. "What?"

She knew he'd heard her. Was he stalling so he could frame his answer? "Do you ever think about leaving Forever and seeing what the rest of the country has to offer?"

"Seriously?"

"Of course, seriously." The grin she saw on his face made her wonder if he still thought she was ultimately kidding.

"Nope."

She stopped walking for a moment and scrutinized his expression. "Really?"

"Really," he confirmed. "This is where I'm supposed to be," he told her, then gave her more of a basic reason for why he felt content here. "Everybody here knows everybody else, looks after everybody else. It's like one big family. We don't always get along, but that's what happens in a family," he said with a shrug. "But the bottom line is that if something comes up, we've all got each other's backs. If I left," he theorized, "that's one less back that's covered—and who's gonna cover mine?" he asked. He supposed that sounded overly syrupy to her. "You probably think that I'm crazy."

Nothing could be further from the truth—although

because of the nature of her work, she'd *had* the opportunity to see the world and discover what it had to offer. "No, actually I think you're lucky."

"Lucky?" he questioned, wondering if she was just patronizing him.

Val nodded. "Lucky," she repeated. "Not that many people have what you feel you have. They spend their whole lives looking to fit in somewhere and you've done it without giving it much effort at all—and never leaving your own backyard. I call that lucky."

He turned the tables on her. "How about you? Do you feel like you fit in where you are?"

Her answer wasn't as quick as his. She gave the matter thought before saying, "For now, yes."

"And later?" he pressed, curious.

"Will come later," she told him elusively. She didn't want to get overly serious about herself. She wanted to keep this relationship—and the information that went into it—light. At least on her end. "C'mon, introduce me to Jack."

"Brett, Liam and Finn," he corrected. "Jack is their father's name. The saloon originally belonged to him."

"So the saloon *did* close down once in a while," she responded with an approving nod of her head.

"What makes you say that?" he asked, curious as to her deduction.

"Simple. Jack Sr. must have had some downtime, otherwise, there wouldn't be a Brett, a Liam and a Finn," Val said.

Jack's was right up in front of them, a small two-story building that was in desperate need of a paint job. The wood had darkened in the sun, looking the way saloons must have looked like at the turn of the *past* century.

Rafe laughed as he opened the door for her. "Nothing gets by you, does it?"

She felt it best not to answer that. Instead, she gave him a mysterious smile as she walked past him. She felt it was more effective that way.

And it was.

## Chapter Eleven

It was dim within the small room that comprised the saloon, although not quite as dim as Val had actually expected.

The interior of Jack's was one-third the size of Miss Joan's diner and the two-story building faced a side street off what could whimsically be referred to as the beaten path. Miss Joan's diner was centrally located, easily gotten to from any corner of the town. Jack's necessitated a definite pilgrimage as well as knowledge of where one was going.

That was done on purpose, some of the town council maintained, to discourage seducing the "young people" and keep them from going in, but the actual case was that the town had just naturally built up around the diner, not the saloon.

The latter was not a social outcast nor a pariah. Each establishment served its own purpose, although some of the wives in Forever and the outlying area felt that Jack's purpose was simply to keep their husbands away from home for large chunks of time.

Still, possibly thanks to the fact that there was a sheriff's department that was not overly busy and welcomed some sort of work, the people who frequented Jack's comprised a relatively quiet crowd. They were far more interested in either socializing or drinking to forget than becoming confrontational, boisterous or troublesome.

When Val and Rafe walked into the establishment, the place was empty except for a tall, lean bartender who was busy putting glasses away behind the bar and his lone customer. The latter could be said to be communing with the bar, his face very obviously pressed against the gleaming, well-polished surface.

The customer was snoring.

The irritatingly loud noise didn't seem to bother the bartender.

When the floorboards creaked beneath their boots, the bartender half turned in their direction to see who had come in. "You here to claim him?" he asked before he'd turned fully around.

"Actually, I'm just here to show Val your den of iniquity," Rafe responded.

Coming forward, Rafe peered at the man sleeping on the counter. There was only half a profile available for examination but it was enough. He recognized the unconscious man.

"You're letting Jamison sleep it off here again?" Rafe asked.

After finishing another glass, the bartender set it down on the bar. Interest gleamed in his eyes as he looked over the woman Rafe had referred to as "Val."

"There's no 'letting' involved," the bartender answered. "I'm doing it to preserve a life. Two, actually.

Jamison's missus said she'd skin us both the next time I brought him home in that condition. So I left him here. Figured Jamison looked better with his skin on."

"But not you?" Val asked, amused by the man's narrative.

Brett Jack turned around completely to face her, then glanced in Rafe's direction, waiting for an official introduction.

"This is Valentine Jones," Rafe told him. "She's out here scouting locations for a movie."

Brett wiped his hands and set the towel on the bar for a moment. "Pleased to meet you, Valentine."

"It's Val," she corrected, making a mental note not to introduce herself using her full name anymore. It was hard to get people to take her seriously at first. "And likewise," Val told him, shaking the hand he held out to her.

"To answer your question," Brett said, picking up the thread of the conversation where he'd dropped it. "I like my skin just where it is, too, but his missus is a little bitty woman. She'd have to catch me to skin me."

"Jamison doesn't exactly look like a lightweight," she pointed out.

"He's not—but he's afraid of his wife," Brett told her.

"And you're not," Val assumed.

"Not a woman alive I'm afraid of," Brett told her matter-of-factly. "Except for my dear, sainted mother, but she's gone now. And for the record," he added, "I never partake when I'm on the job. You never know what might come up."

She supposed, given the nature of his work, that was

a wise position to take. She nodded at the sleeping customer. "Does Mr. Jamison do this all the time?"

"You mean drink himself into a stupor and then sleep it off on my bar?" She nodded. "Only when he's got money in his pocket," Brett told her.

Definitely colorful, she thought. "And he doesn't mind sleeping like that?" she asked out loud. All she could think of was the way the man's neck was going to ache when he woke up.

Brett shook his head. "Says he likes to be close to his supply of alcohol. To each his own. I guess."

Still, that had to be awfully uncomfortable, she judged. Val looked at Rafe. "Shouldn't you bring him home?"

Rafe raised his hands slightly, as if to fend off the thought. "I don't relish getting skinned any more than Brett here does."

"But his wife could see that you haven't been drinking, which means that you weren't around him when he was drinking, so you're not responsible for his condition," she argued.

"That would be a reasonable deduction," Rafe agreed, "but Jamison's missus isn't exactly known for being reasonable. What do you think he's drinking to forget?" he asked her.

She looked from the man behind the bar to Rafe. The answer to Rafe's question was suddenly as obvious as the shine on the bar.

"Oh." She looked at Jamison. The man's snoring was getting louder. "I guess his neck won't hurt too much when he wakes up."

"Not as much as the welts he'd have on his body once Charlene got hold of him," Brett guaranteed. "Don't worry, I'll water down his drinks for the first part of the day when he starts in again—and charge him accordingly," he said.

Leaving the rest of the glasses where they were, Brett crossed his arms before him as he took a closer look at the woman Rafe had brought into the establishment he co-owned with his brothers.

"Did I hear Rafe right earlier? Are you looking for a place to make a movie?"

"Actually, I'm not looking anymore," she answered. "The deal's already been finalized. We'll be bringing our production company here within the next few days. Miss Joan and the town council voted on it and agreed it would be all right with everyone."

Brett laughed shortly. "Miss Joan *is* the town council. Can't think of a single time that woman was for or against something and got opposed by someone on the council, never mind voted down by the *whole* council. They know better than that." The bartender seemed to roll the idea of a film crew mingling with the local citizens over in his head. "So she actually *likes* the idea of a whole bunch of strangers coming into Forever, disrupting everything? How'd you manage to talk her into that?" he marveled. "I'm assuming that you're the one who did the talking," he added.

"I didn't talk her into it," Val protested, although not too vehemently. "What I did was promise her that nothing would be damaged—if it was, we'd definitely pay to have it fixed or replaced—and that the town would be given a sizeable sum of money in exchange for the use of the area." She noticed the skeptical look on the bartender's broad, handsome face. "You don't believe me." It wasn't a question, it was a conclusion.

Brett shrugged his broad shoulders. "No disrespect intended, ma'am, but on occasion, when things are particularly slow, I do thumb through those Hollywood tell-all rags they've got at the grocery store," he told her, referring to the tabloids that had a way of turning up absolutely everywhere, like dust on unattended furniture. "From what I read, Hollywood people love to party and while that might be good for *my* business, that kind of thing can't ultimately be good for the town." He looked at her for another long moment. "No offense, but if I'd been at the meeting, I'd have voted no."

"See what you miss by not coming to the meetings?" Rafe pointed out, doing his best not to grin.

Brett frowned. "Usually, it's a snooze fest, two people jawing for hours, debating whether or not the sign outside the town could stand to be repainted and if it did, what color to make it, that sort of thing," he explained for Val's benefit. "Doesn't really excite me," he concluded. "When did you say your people were coming?" he asked her.

The way he phrased it, it made her feel as if she was the standard bearer for the entire movie industry. That, and an outsider, as well. An unwelcome outsider.

"The production company'll be here as soon as they can get everyone together." Because she could see that he was waiting for an actual number, she made an estimate based on her past experiences. "Anywhere from a couple of days to a couple of weeks. Nothing happens fast in our industry," she confided, making the admission to Rafe rather than the bartender. "Our overall motto unfortunately is hurry up and wait."

"That's funny," Brett told her, his mouth curving in amusement.

Well, at least someone was amused, she thought. As for her, she'd be a whole lot happier if things could proceed at least a little faster. She knew that Jim felt the same way she did. But it was hard to light a fire under so many people and movie making took intense coordination. Still, the films that Jim had a hand in usually came in ahead of schedule as well as under budget. That was why, most of the time, the man had no difficulty in finding financial backing.

"Sadly, it's also true," she told Brett.

As if he suddenly remembered his chosen vocation, Brett straightened just a tad behind the bar and asked, "Would you like a drink? On the house?" he added before she could answer.

"Maybe later," Val responded.

She wasn't much on social drinking and when she did imbibe, it tended to be some kind of a mixed, fruity drink, the kind that hit her knees, made her talk faster for a few minutes and then faded away. She had a feeling that the bartender at Jack's would look down at something like that—if he actually knew how to prepare those kinds of drinks.

Even if she was given to drinking something harder, it was a little early in the day to start consuming alcohol.

She turned toward Rafe. "Right now, I believe I owe you a steak."

Brett's dark eyes slid over Val's frame slowly, then glanced over toward Rafe. A knowing half smile curved his mouth.

"Lucky guy," he commented.

Rafe had a hunch that Brett thought something more than a meal was being discussed at the moment. He also knew that if he protested in any manner—for Val's sake—it would only add weight to what Brett was already mistakenly thinking.

To be honest, Rafe had no idea why he felt this overwhelming desire to defend her honor, especially since they hardly knew one another. In all likelihood, Valentine Jones was probably involved with someone in Hollywood. And he knew that it would take more than a protest from him to change Brett's mind.

So instead, he merely nodded and said, "Yeah, I guess I am. Miss Joan gets her meat from the best cattle ranchers." He didn't bother adding that his family's ranch numbered among them. That would sound like bragging. "See you around," Rafe said to the bartender just as he followed Val out.

The sun felt warmer to her as they began to walk back to the diner. Since this was Texas, she'd expected it to be much colder here in January than it was back home. But, she reminded herself, this was the southern part of Texas and as such, given to more temperate weather. She found that fortunate since she'd never cared for cold weather in general.

She glanced back at Rafe, who caught up to her in a

couple more steps. "He thinks I'm sleeping with you, doesn't he?" she asked.

The question, coming out of the blue like that, took Rafe by surprise. This woman was a wee bit more abrupt, not to mention honest, than he was accustomed to—if he didn't include his sister, Alma. Alma had an in-your-face kind of attitude when it came to the men in the family.

But Val wasn't family and he wasn't sure just how to respond to her question. Rafe looked at her for a long moment, searching for a way to answer her. Not many things left him speechless, but this question certainly had.

"Yeah, I think he does," he finally heard himself tell her. Honesty was always the best way to go—especially if you didn't have a game plan and didn't want to trip up.

"Why didn't you set him straight?" There was no indignation in her voice.

What he heard, again to his surprise, was just plain curiosity. So rather than come up with some half-baked excuse, Rafe went with his instincts and told her the truth.

"Because I thought if I told Brett I wasn't—that we weren't—" He decided not to frame that part of the conversation. She knew what he was getting at, he silently argued. "—he'd just think I was lying. You know, that famous line about someone protesting too much, that sort of thing."

"And that's the only reason?" she asked, cocking her head and studying him.

"What other reason is there?" he asked.

That seemed like a simple enough deduction to her. "Well, by not saying anything, you might have thought he'd think that we *were* sleeping together and you'd have bragging rights."

"Not that sleeping with you wouldn't be something to really brag about," Rafe qualified, "but I've always found that if you lie about something, somehow, some way, some day, that lie comes back and bites you on the—well, it bites you where you don't want to be bitten."

Rafe saw the grin that spread out across her lips. Was she laughing at him? Or was that just her reaction to not believing him?

"What?" he asked. It seemed like even her eyes were laughing.

"Seems we've got something in common, Rafe. I don't lie or stretch the truth for the same reason—and because I don't want to be lied to myself and I certainly don't want to be caught in a lie. Maybe I'm naive, but I'd like to think that if I always tell the truth, aside from having people believe me when I tell them something, they also feel guilty if they lie to me—and so to keep their consciences clear, they don't."

She saw the diner come into view as they turned down another street. She changed the subject to something more pleasant. "So, how do you like your steak?" she asked him cheerfully.

"Barely dead," Rafe answered automatically.

When the words were out of his mouth, he realized what that had to sound like to her. He expected her to make a face. After all, didn't all California girls espouse eating only vegetables and turn their noses up at anything that didn't have the word "green" in it?

Instead, he saw her grin again—and had the same reaction that he'd had the first time—and every time. Because each time he saw her grin like that, he felt his stomach muscles quickening. They seemed to be doing it faster and faster.

Rather than growing more immune to her, he discovered that he was growing more susceptible to her. That couldn't be good. Ultimately, this couldn't go anywhere. He was treading on a slippery path, but somehow, he couldn't seem to reason himself into staying clear of the path—and her.

Since he wasn't altogether certain what she was grinning about, he asked for an explanation. "What?"

"That's the exact same way I like my steak. Barely dead," she repeated. "My mother's convinced I'm going to wind up ingesting tapeworms or something equally as unhealthy and dangerous one day."

"Hasn't happened to me yet and I've eaten more than my share of steaks," he told her, holding the door to the diner open for her.

"I'll be sure to cite you as a reference the next time my mother starts in on how bad that kind of a meal is for me," she told him just before she walked into the diner.

He had no idea why something like that—being used to defend her stand as well as convince her mother—would make him smile, but it did.

Rafe was beginning to discover that everything about this woman was making him smile.

## Chapter Twelve

"Wow. I didn't think it was possible, but this place is even more perfect close up than in those photographs you sent me," Jim Sinclair said enthusiastically as he surveyed the town.

He and his crew had arrived with their trailers just a short while ago, parking the vehicles as unobtrusively as possible on the far side of town.

Not that far, coincidentally, from the saloon.

The moment she saw him, Val had brought the director right into the center of Forever. She'd been told the other day that, at Christmastime, the people of the town would gather together around the tall pine tree that was selected each year and they would all take turns decorating.

As she stood beside Jim, Val could almost see an eighteen-foot tree, decked out in all its glory, a point of pride for everyone in Forever and a symbol of the citizens' inherent goodwill.

Val smiled to herself. She was willing to bet that the whole thing was a good deal like an old-fashioned 1940s musical come to life.

For just a moment, she couldn't help wondering what it had to have been like for Rafe, growing up in a town like this. And maybe, just for that moment, she'd even envied him.

Not that she hadn't had a good childhood herself, Val quickly amended. She'd grown up loved, wanting for nothing and playing with the children of A-list celebrities—not that the last part mattered all that much to her. What mattered then—as it did now—was whether or not the people she associated with were good people and fun to be with.

Taking it all in, Jim slipped his arm around her shoulders and gave her a quick, intense half hug. To the unobservant eye, Jim Sinclair looked like a gangly, slightly-too-thin, recent college graduate eager to make his mark on the world. Only upon closer scrutiny did it become obvious that Jim was actually a lot older than he appeared. There was just the barest hint of gray in his sandy-colored hair and a few lines had crept in around his mouth—smile lines, he liked to call them, because Jim loved his work, loved knowing that he was reaching so many people.

Was he Val's boyfriend? Not that it really mattered, Rafe told himself, hanging back. After all, the woman would be gone the moment the movie was finished being filmed. Maybe even sooner.

There was absolutely no kind of future for him with her.

But nonetheless, he watched the tall, thin man's movements intently.

It had taken more than a week for the film crew to

come out and for most of the time while she was waiting for the crew to arrive, when his father didn't have
him doing something on the ranch, Rafe would spend
the time with Val. He showed her the different sights,
got to know her a little better and found himself inevi-
tably getting closer to her.

He tried to downplay the latter in his mind now,
telling himself that she was an exceptionally attractive
young woman and he was just doing what came naturally. But the truth of it was, he wasn't all that sure it
was only that, because the intensity of what he was feeling toward her was of a caliber that he had never experienced before. For that matter, he'd never felt a single
glimmer of jealousy about any of the girls and women
he'd been with prior to Val—and technically, he wasn't
even actually *with* her. He was just occupying space
in the same area that she was, he silently argued. That
didn't qualify as any kind of a relationship.

He was losing the argument, he realized. That was
*not* exactly an encouraging thing when the opponent
was himself.

"You know, the sun doesn't go down for hours,"
Mike said, coming up behind him as the crowd around
the newly arrived film crew started to grow, lured there
by curiosity.

Caught off guard, Rafe turned around. He hadn't
even noticed that his oldest brother was in the vicinity, much less right behind him—and spouting riddles.

"Why would I care when the sun goes down?" Rafe
asked, confused.

"Well, when the sun goes down," Mike told him,

pushing the brim of his hat back with the tip of his thumb, "it gets dark, and that way, you can hang out in the shadows, observing things to your heart's content without running the risk of being seen by the person you're watching."

Rafe frowned. "You're not making any sense," he told Mike dismissively.

"Well," Mike decided, "that makes two of us. Because it sure doesn't make any sense to hang back the way you are, just glaring at that tall, skinny guy with his arm around Val. If it bothers you so much to see that, go up and stake your claim."

Now Rafe was certain that his brother wasn't making any sense. "Stake my claim? She's not a piece of property, she's a woman."

Mike gripped his brother by the shoulders, as if that could somehow make him see the light faster. "Exactly. The woman you've been seeing ever since you brought her over to the house to make that pitch to use our ranch for the movie. Don't just hang back and let this Hollywood guy snatch her away from you."

With Mike, things were always so black and white. But they weren't like that in the real world, Rafe thought.

"In case you haven't noticed, she's from Hollywood, too, or thereabouts," Rafe qualified. He realized that he wasn't all that certain exactly just where Val called home.

"Well, don't hold that against her, little brother," Mike told him. "After all, the girl had no say over where she was born and raised."

Rafe laughed and shook his head. "You're crazy, you know that, right?"

Mike looked at him, a serious expression taking over his features. "Not half as crazy as you if you just let her go like that."

A skeptical look came over Rafe's face. "Since when have you become such an advocate of what a guy's supposed to do if he wants to hang on to a woman—which I don't, by the way."

"I read a lot," Mike replied drily. "And as for the rest of what you just said—bull," he declared with more than just a touch of earnest conviction. "I'm your older brother and I know you pretty much inside and out. You're sweet on that girl and for what it's worth, you two *do* kind of look good together."

Rafe laughed shortly. "Oh, well, as long as you approve, everything's perfect," he said loftily, sarcasm dripping from every syllable.

"Get off your high horse, Rafe. I'm just looking out for you. She needs work," his brother admitted, "but all in all, I've changed my opinion about her. She's not half bad, really. God knows you could do a whole lot worse."

Who was he to pass judgment on Val? Rafe could feel his temper flaring. "Why don't you just butt out of my business?"

"Glad to," Mike answered. "Just as soon as you butt into it," he told Rafe.

Rafe stared at him. "What the hell's that supposed to mean?"

"It means start taking charge. Head's up, now's your

chance," Mike announced as he nodded at something just behind his brother.

"What are you talking about now?" Rafe asked in exasperation as he turned around.

He found himself looking at Val and her director's thin, shallow chest. To look into Jim Sinclair's gaunt face required looking up. For a second, Rafe was speechless, but that made no difference because Val had taken over and was now doing the talking.

"Jim, this is the guy I was telling you about." Shifting positions, she hooked her arm through Rafe's, gently nudging him forward. Neither one of them noticed Mike stepping back and out of their circle. "Rafe Rodriguez. My tour guide," she added with a really wide smile as she looked up into Rafe's face.

"Nice to meet you," Jim said warmly, extending his rather large hand to the man beside Val.

During his senior year in high school, so the story went, Jim had spent five agonizing months, trying to decide whether his heart belonged to basketball or filmmaking. He'd played well enough to be offered a sports scholarship to a midwestern college, but ultimately he went with filmmaking. He enrolled in a local university, went after a degree in films and never looked back, luckily for the audiences who wholeheartedly enjoyed his movies.

"Since you've been so helpful to Val," Jim told him, "how would you feel about staying on as a consultant while we're filming here? Full salary, of course," he added.

Rafe looked at the director uncertainly, convinced he'd heard wrong. "You want to *pay* me?"

"Yes. For being a consultant," Jim repeated. "Would that be all right with you?"

He knew that his younger brother would have jumped at this chance to hang around the set while they were filming—and get paid to boot—but Rafe didn't want to just take the man's money without knowing what was expected of him.

"And exactly what would I have to do as a 'consultant?'" Rafe honestly had no idea what something like that involved.

"Be consulted," Jim replied with a straight face that cracked into a grin halfway through. "Just kidding. But what you *would* do is answer questions about the area if we need anything." His expression indicated that he knew he wasn't really being very clear on the subject. "Sorry, but it doesn't get any more specific than that," Jim apologized. "But I could really use someone local to be a go-between between the good people of Forever and my crew. Make sure things are running smoothly and let us know if maybe we're overstepping some sort of boundaries.

"Maybe we should call you a good will ambassador instead." Jim laughed. "For starters, Val probably already told you that we're also going to need a lot of the citizens here to be in our street shots, lend some authenticity to the movie. You could point us in the right direction, tell us who we could use and who might be a little hard to work with." Jim lowered his voice, making their conversation seem exceedingly personal as he added, "Sometimes people get carried away, play up to the camera, that sort of thing. We need people who can be natural, ignore the cameras around them, understand what I mean?" Jim asked.

Rafe had his doubts about this. "Val said that the movie was supposed to be taking place in like the late '60s."

"It does," Jim confirmed. "Is there a problem with that?"

"Well, just off the top of my head, I don't think anyone here's got the kind of clothes you would have seen back then just hanging around in their closets."

"Good point," Jim agreed, treating the argument seriously. "That's where the wardrobe department comes in. We've brought enough clothes with us to outfit as many people as we're going to need."

That still didn't fix things, Rafe thought. "No offense, but the folks here don't exactly come in the standard, thin Hollywood size," he pointed out.

"Let you in on a secret," Jim said. "Neither do the Hollywood 'folks.' Not to worry," he added. "We've got people who can make those adjustments, take in clothes or let them out, as needed. Anything else?"

"Can't think of anything at the moment," Rafe admitted, beginning to take a liking to the man despite himself.

"So does that mean you'll take the job? Be our consultant/liaison?" Jim asked.

He supposed it sounded simple enough. And, Rafe assumed, it *would* allow him to hang around Val a bit more closely. "Sure, why not?"

"Great," Jim enthused, clapping his hands together. "Now, where's your mayor?" he asked, scanning the immediate area, presumably for someone who looked the part of a small-town mayor. "I need to get the contract giving us permission to film here signed so we can issue the town a check and get that all out of the way."

Rafe was about to say that they didn't really have an official building where the mayor did business. Harold Chesterfield won the past election uncontested mainly because no one wanted the extra work. The title was more or less an honorary one, the position paying a few extra hundred dollars a year. Chesterfield worked out of his own home, conducting official business in his den. Any meetings took place in Miss Joan's diner.

But before Rafe could explain any of this, he saw the portly man breaking through the ever-growing crowd of people.

With the instincts of a homing pigeon, Chesterfield was making his way over.

"That's him right there," Rafe said. He nodded toward the approaching mayor. Jim turned to see whom he was referring to. "His name's Harold Chesterfield."

That was about all Rafe had time to say before the mayor and his wife descended on the film director and the handful of people he'd brought with him for this first look around the town.

Rafe stepped back, getting out of the way. He had a hunch that the director wouldn't be needing his further "services" at the moment.

To his surprise, Val stepped back with him rather than remain with the director.

"Aren't you supposed to be with him?" Rafe asked.

"I'd rather be with you," she answered before she could give her answer any thought. "Jim can handle this on his own," she continued, hoping Rafe would focus on this part. "I've seen him charm a whole town before. Audrey says that he could get along with the devil with no effort if he had to."

She'd sprung a new name on him. Or was he already supposed to know this one? "Audrey?"

Val nodded. "Jim's wife."

"He's married?" Rafe asked, doing his best to keep the relief he was suddenly experiencing out of his voice. But he had to admit that he felt a whole lot more inclined to smile right now than he had a few minutes ago.

"For the past eleven years," she told him. "Audrey was the star of Jim's very first feature film. He always likes to say she took direction so well, he married her." Val always smiled at the old familiar quote. "When the kids started coming along, she decided to give up her career and focus her attention on her family."

Rafe was still stuck in first gear—but as far as he was concerned, it was a great gear to be stuck in. "So he's married, huh?"

Humor curved her mouth. "I thought we already established that part. Audrey's a terrific lady." She looked at him more closely, picking up more in his tone and his expression than he would have wanted her to. "Did you think that he and I…?" And then, before she could finish the sentence, she began to laugh.

Second guessing what she was about to ask—

because he'd been so focused on just this particular aspect—Rafe shifted uncomfortably.

"No, why would I?" he protested possibly a little too stringently. She was still laughing. "Why are you laughing?" he asked.

She hooked her arm through his and moved him even farther away from the center of the growing crowd. "Because I think you're sweet." Then, before he could protest an image he didn't care for, she quickly continued. "And because Jim's like the older brother I never had. He looks out for me. I used to babysit his kids when they were really little. Now he and I work together. And when we 'play' together," Val specified, "it's *really* playing and usually his family's on the set and involved in whatever the game is. Jim's a real family man. He likes having his wife and kids close whenever possible. It's hard being a family man in this industry," she confided, knowing firsthand the problems her own parents had endured, "but Jim's managed to make it work." Pausing, she smiled at him before asking, "Do you have any other questions for me?"

"I didn't even have that one," Rafe pointed out stiffly, feeling embarrassed that he was apparently so transparent to her.

"Yes, you did," she countered with a warm smile. "And I'm flattered. For the record, I am *not* involved with anyone. In the interest of full disclosure, I was married once, though." She saw him look at her in surprise.

"Was," Rafe repeated, watching her expression. "But you're not now."

"No."

For once, she didn't elaborate and he found that rather odd. "What happened?" The moment he uttered the question, he realized how intrusive and insensitive that had probably sounded to her. He had no right to be prying like this. Most likely, she didn't want to talk about it. Most people with failed marriages preferred to ignore the whole episode. "Sorry, none of my business."

"He died," Val replied quietly, her eyes meeting his.

"Oh. I'm sorry," he said with sincerity.

She supposed the first sentence was the hardest. Now that she had uttered it, she might as well tell him the rest of it. After all, she wasn't ashamed of loving Scott, or of marrying him.

"He was a stuntman. We got married way too young and there were a few bumps in the road, a few things that needed to be ironed out," she told him honestly, "but I think it might have worked out in the long run. He was a good guy," Val said fondly. "But he was a little reckless and stunt work isn't exactly the place for that sort of cavalier attitude."

As she talked, they walked farther away from the crowd. This was something personal and she was sharing it with one specific person. She didn't care to be overheard. There were people in the crew—of course Jim—who knew her circumstances, but she was in no mood for either questions or sympathy from those who didn't.

"A gag went wrong," she said simply.

"Gag?" Rafe repeated, trying to follow what she was

telling him. "You mean like a joke he pulled?" He tried to think of a practical joke that could go so badly.

She flashed an apologetic smile at him. "Sorry, I forget sometimes that everyone wasn't raised on a movie set like I was. A 'gag' is what insiders call a stunt. He was supposed to flip a car, you know, one of those chase scenes they're always doing and trying to make bigger, better, more exciting. More daring and dangerous. Well, Scott thought it would be 'more daring' if he was in the car for longer than he was supposed to be.

"The stunt was supposed to stop short of the car going into a roll and he was 'supposed' to get out," she said, stretching the word. "Except that he didn't and the controlled roll got way out of hand…" For a moment, the words stuck in her throat, but then she continued. "The car burst into flames and Scott was trapped."

She pressed her lips together, getting her voice under control and then went on. "The medical examiner told me that he'd been killed instantly—but I still have nightmares about that fire. About his last few seconds…" She drew in a breath and then released it slowly.

Rafe watched as she straightened and lifted her chin, managing to shed the serious mood that had all but enshrouded her.

"C'mon," she suddenly said brightly, taking his hand in hers and moving back toward the center of the crowd. "I'll introduce you around. They're a great group of people," she assured him.

But Rafe held her back for a second. He wanted to get in one final private word before they stepped back into what was decidedly her world. "I didn't mean to stir up bad memories for you."

"You didn't," she told him, grateful for this display of his sensitivity. "That's just all part of my life and it's in the past. But I don't ever want to forget Scott. We had a good year and a half together," she told him. "And I wouldn't have traded it for the world. Now c'mon." she tugged on his hand. "If you're going to be Jim's 'consultant' there are people you need to meet and know by name." She winked at him before turning forward and pulling him in her wake.

He went willingly. It was at that point that he realized he would have followed her to the ends of the earth—or into the jaws of hell—if that was what she wanted.

But he still refused to explore *why*.

## Chapter Thirteen

"Is this what it's like?" Rafe raised his voice as he asked Val the question more than a week later.

On a whim, they had walked into Miss Joan's diner to grab a bite to eat and found that the place was unbelievably crowded. Rafe couldn't recall *ever* seeing the diner filled to this capacity. It was all but bulging at the seams.

Not only that, but there were more than a few people lined up next to the register, waiting for someone to leave so that seats could be vacated and they could finally sit down. Thinking back, over the years, even at the height of the business day, Rafe couldn't remember the diner being *this* busy.

Leaning into him so that he could hear her, unaware of the chaos she was creating to his insides by being so very close, Val raised her own voice and asked, "Is *what* like?"

"Life where you come from. In the city," he added in case he was still being unclear. "Is it always this crowded so that you can't hear yourself think?"

This was nothing in comparison to some of the

crowded conditions she'd encountered, she thought. To her, it was no big deal, and she answered Rafe's question with a careless shrug.

"I guess."

In all honesty, she was accustomed to waiting, to inching her way from one destination to another on one of many Southern California freeways, which like as not usually alternated between a crawl and a complete stop. Free-flowing traffic was reserved for the absolute dead of night or very early Sunday mornings.

"Although," she continued, "Hollywood isn't nearly as bad as New York City. There it's the streets that are exceedingly crowded. In Hollywood, it's the freeways. For the most part, walking is a lost art in L.A., although there are still some of us diehards left." She smiled at him. "But in comparison to what you would find in that city, this is nothing," she assured him, gesturing around the diner.

Silently, she had to admit that she was a little surprised to see how full the diner actually was. Especially since Miss Joan's was no longer the only place in town to get food. The production company had its own catering truck and each day, more than enough food was flown in to provide three square meals for the cast and crew, with a good margin so that there would be leftovers to snack on, should there be the need.

However, the makeshift commissary that had been set up beneath a wide, open-ended tent was usually empty most of the time. Word had spread about the food in Miss Joan's diner and, one by one, the skeptics had come to sample and the converts returned on a daily basis. They were all here, rubbing elbows with the locals.

It disgruntled the regulars, some of whom voiced their displeasure where others could hear, saying that they couldn't wait until "these outsiders took themselves back to wherever it was that they came from. And the sooner, the better."

Overhearing the last statement, Miss Joan stopped what she was doing and made her way over to where the offending party was standing, waiting for a seat. Among her other duties, she had always considered herself to be a peacemaker, disarming frays before they could become either dangerous or emotionally damaging.

"Now, Bill," she began reprovingly, like a maiden aunt focused on restoring good manners to a favored nephew, "someone hearing you would say that you weren't being neighborly."

Bill, a towering, heavyset man in his late forties frowned. "Someone hearing me would also hear my stomach grumbling and understand," the weather-beaten wrangler complained, glaring at the four men who had just taken a newly freed-up table.

"We'll get you something to go," Miss Joan told him, patting his arm as if the wrangler was a petulant child who needed to be reminded of the boundaries. "And a big piece of my peach pie, as well," she whispered. "On the house."

Rafe wouldn't have overheard the bribe if he hadn't been standing right next to the complaining wrangler. "Seems to me you got the better end of the deal," he told the man called Bill.

Bill muttered something unintelligible under his breath.

Ignoring him, Miss Joan turned and seemed to see Rafe and the woman with him for the first time. Her ordinarily sedate features lit up considerably. She was almost beaming. It was an expression most in town weren't familiar with.

"Rita," she called out to one of the waitresses she'd put on extra shifts to handle the overflow of customers. "Take care of Bill here." Returning her attention to the two people standing beside her, Miss Joan slipped one arm through each one of theirs and announced, "No need for the two of you to stand around, waiting. Come with me. I've set aside a table for two just in case either one of you decided to come in."

Rafe and Val exchanged looks, but neither of them was more in the know than the other.

"What's the occasion?" Rafe asked Miss Joan. While he didn't mind getting preferential treatment once in a while, he didn't like the idea of just pushing his way past other people in order to be served first. That was just plain unfair.

"No occasion," Miss Joan replied. "I'm just expressing my gratitude to the young lady who made all this extra business and change in my pocket possible." Her usually thin-lipped, small smile was spread to its ultimate stretching point as she added, "At the very least, this'll allow me to buy a really nice gift for the grandbaby who's coming."

It took Rafe a second to replay her words in his head.

When he did, he stared at Miss Joan, stunned. "*What* grandbaby?" he asked.

Miss Joan had married Harry Monroe a while back and Harry's grandson, Cash Taylor, had returned to Forever for the wedding. Once Miss Joan married Harry, Cash became her step-grandson. Rafe recalled that Cash and his sister, Alma, had once been sweethearts until Cash had gone away to college. Alma was supposed to have attended the same school, but because the family ranch was facing possible foreclosure at the time, she'd stayed behind to help out by taking on a job.

When Cash came back for his grandfather's wedding, the romance reignited. The upshot was that Cash wound up staying and marrying Rafe's sister. Cash would be Miss Joan's only source of a grandchild—which in turn meant—

Rafe's eyes widened so far that they all but fell out of his head. "Alma's pregnant?"

"She didn't tell you?" It was hard to judge by Miss Joan's expression whether the woman was surprised, or if she knew that she was among the first to have the news and was just teasing him in her droll way. "Guess it must have slipped her mind. She'll tell you in her own time," Miss Joan promised, then winked. "When she does, don't let on that you already know. Now then," the woman continued as the pair seated themselves at the table she'd brought them to, "you two know what you want or should I come back?"

"Is Angel cooking today?" Rafe asked, referring to Gabe's fiancée.

"Angel is *always* cooking," Miss Joan replied with a throaty laugh.

"Great, then I'll have whatever her special is today," Rafe replied. His future sister-in-law had the ability to make a stone taste tempting.

"That would be the pot roast," Miss Joan told him after glancing over her shoulder at the counter where a sign informing her customers of that day's special was posted.

Angel's cooking had gained such favor that had she said her special was a pile of nails swimming in water, she would have received the same enthusiastic response. In a very short amount of time, people who frequented Miss Joan's diner had fallen under the spell of the magic that Angel performed every day in Miss Joan's kitchen.

"Make that two," Val told her. "And I'd love a cola if you have one."

"For you, anything," Miss Joan said with all due sincerity. Her business had always been decent, but what had been going on lately was close to unbelievable. And she was a woman who always paid her dues and made sure she expressed her gratitude. "And by the way, it's on the house."

"No," Val protested. "You can't get money for a special gift for that grandbaby of yours if you give the food away."

When she made up her mind, Miss Joan never changed it. "Trust me, I can. Besides, it's only in your case. And Harry's of course."

"Harry's?" Val asked, curious.

"Harry Monroe. My husband," Miss Joan told her.

"I told 'im there were advantages to sleeping with the owner. Free food being one of them."

"The woman is really something else," Val said to Rafe with a laugh. Miss Joan had only taken a few steps away from their table but already the wall of noise had swallowed up her words, so that Val felt fairly certain that the owner of the diner couldn't hear what she'd said.

Rafe leaned forward for the exact same reason, so that she could hear him. "She's a regular pistol, according to Harry," he said.

Sitting forward like this, leaning into Val so that she could hear him, made Rafe acutely aware of all the things that made her so attractive to him. The scent of her hair, the way her eyes seemed to smile with some secret joke all their own, the creamy complexion that tempted him to reach out and touch her just to prove to himself that she wasn't some fanciful dream he was having. A dream that would break up into so many pieces the second he did reach out.

With effort, he kept his hands where they were, resting on the table. He didn't want to risk spoiling the moment, even though he could feel a growing ache inside of him that had nothing to do with eating.

"I guess Miss Joan is really happy about all this chaos," Val assumed as she looked around the filled-beyond-capacity diner.

The makeshift commissary, which could accommodate more than twice as many people as the diner, was all but empty when she'd passed by it earlier.

"Chaos means money, so yes, I'm sure Miss Joan is happy. I heard that the man who runs the grocery store as well as the couple who own the town's only clothing store are all beside themselves with all this extra business you brought into this town."

"I have nothing to do with it," Val protested. "Those photos of your ranch and of this town are what lured Jim and his film company out here. They deserve all the credit."

"Yes," he said, raising his voice again as the crowd grew even noisier, "but you're the one who took the photographs," he reminded her. "If you hadn't had such a good eye for what your boss wanted, none of this would be happening," he concluded very simply.

Miss Joan returned, carrying a tray with two complete pot roast dinners. Rather than turning the order over to one of her waitresses, she made a point to wait on them personally.

"You be sure to let me know if there's anything else you want," the woman reminded them before hurrying back to oversee her section of the counter.

As Miss Joan retreated, Rafe caught a little of her triumphant smile. "I don't think I've ever seen the woman this happy, even at her wedding."

Val smiled, pleased. "Full coffers have a way of doing that to a person," she told him.

He nodded his agreement. There was definitely no arguing with that.

"Tell me," he said as he began to make short work of a pot roast that all but melted in his mouth, "how did you wind up being a location scout? Or was that something you always wanted to be?"

Val refrained from laughing at the question. To her

knowledge, no one ever woke up one morning and decided to become a location scout. It was just one of those things that just happened.

"Actually," she said out loud, "I majored in photography in college."

"With an eye out to work on a film crew?" Rafe guessed.

Because Miss Joan wasn't letting them pay for this, Rafe knew he wasn't about to ask for seconds, so he savored what he was consuming, doing his best to eat slowly. It went against the grain of his usual behavior. For the most part, he usually ate fast so he could get to the next thing he was supposed to be doing.

"With an eye out to take photographs," Val corrected. "I wasn't sure where I'd go from there, be a photojournalist or just someone who wanders the world, snapping interesting photographs that eventually turn into an oversize book that sits on a coffee table, collecting dust.

"But photography in general is rather an uncertain way to make a living and I had been raised to pull my own weight. I used to babysit for Jim Sinclair, and when he happened to see some of my work," she continued, "he offered me a job scouting out locations for him on the project he was developing. I got along well with Jim—he was a friend of my parents' long before I worked for him—and the job sounded interesting." She grinned. "It also paid a *lot* better than babysitting, so I said yes."

"And the rest is history," Rafe concluded with a grin, uttering the time-old cliché.

"Or at least a footnote to it," she allowed with a self-depreciating laugh that he found both enticing and endearing. "By the way," she said, easing into a related topic, "your brother Ray is working out very well. Jim's even giving him a line of dialogue to deliver."

He was almost finished with his meal. It amazed him how fast it could disappear. Or maybe it was the company he was keeping that made time feel as if it was whizzing by.

"A whole line, huh?" he marveled with amusement.

She knew that he was unaware of the way the pay scale worked. "Hey, the pay jumps if you have a speaking part," she told him. "I heard he was hamming it up a little in the beginning, but it seems Ray got the hang of it pretty quickly."

"One line is hardly a speaking part," Rafe couldn't help commenting.

"Oh, but it is. That's the criteria they use."

"Criteria?" he asked.

She nodded. "One line and you go from being an 'extra' to a 'supporting actor.'"

"Just like that?" He couldn't help marveling. Strange rules they had in her world, Rafe thought.

"Just like that," she confirmed.

"Well, good for Ray," Rafe told her. "But, to be honest, I'm more interested in hearing if my father has become a problem yet."

The question, coming out of the blue, mystified her. "Why would your sweet, wonderful father become a problem?" she asked. There were times, when she was growing up, that her own father had seemed too driven, too wrapped up in his work to realize that he was neglecting his relationship with his only daughter.

Those were the times when she would have killed to have a father who was so involved in his kids' lives, who apparently, from what she'd gathered from Rafe and from Alma when she and the deputy had occasion to talk, put his children first every single time. "Your dad's a sweetheart."

"Well, ever since you introduced him to your mother, he's like a teenager with a huge crush. I was just afraid he might have, you know, gone a little overboard, started following her around like a faithful puppy—or come across like a potential stalker," he added, watching her expression.

"Don't worry," she assured him. "Mom said he's a perfect gentleman, courtly and charming every time they interact. And between you and me," Val confided, "it does my mother's ego good to meet such a devoted fan, especially since he flatters her the way he does. It helps my mother relive her glory days—no pun intended," she quickly added, afraid it sounded like a play on her mother's first name. "As a matter of fact, I thought I'd drop in on her after lunch, see how she's doing. Maybe bring her a sandwich from here." Val smiled, recalling something. "She's still talking about the Reuben sandwich she had last Friday. The fact that someone here could recreate something so typical New York-y right here in Texas really impressed her."

"Well, once Angel found out the ingredients, throwing it all together wasn't exactly a Herculean feat," he pointed out. His brother's fiancée was one of the most soft-spoken, mild-mannered women he'd ever known, but she had a fierce competitive streak and hated admitting defeat in anything, even something so simple as recreating a sandwich she'd never heard of.

"Still, my mother appreciated it," Val told him. "Especially since she knew it had taken some effort on Angel's part."

Her mother wasn't one of those people who just accepted things or took them for granted, she made it a point to delve into them, to find out how things came about.

A fond look came over her features as she thought of her mother.

"I found out that she grew up in a little town in Idaho that wasn't much bigger than this one," she told Rafe. "Seeing her now, it's hard for me to imagine that her roots go back to some place so down to earth." *Like here,* she added silently. "My first memory of my mother was seeing her in a sparkling, floor-length silver gown. I thought she was some kind of a queen—which of course made me a princess," she added with a mischievous grin.

"Of course," he echoed. "And I bet you made one hell of a princess."

"Actually, I lasted about seven seconds as a princess. I was more of a tomboy type," she admitted. "I made my mother crazy," she confided. "She'd get me all dressed up in frills and laces for church and I'd get dirty in record time once the service was over."

He leaned back in his chair for a moment, his eyes skimming over her appreciatively. "Well, you certainly cleaned up nicely."

Val laughed. "Don't let the skirt and high heels fool

you. Beneath all this camouflage still beats the heart of a tomboy."

"Beneath all the clothes, huh? I'd like to find that out for myself," he murmured under his breath, thinking she couldn't hear him because of all the surrounding noise and the fact that he was leaning back.

He thought wrong.

## Chapter Fourteen

Val made no comment. Nonetheless, she could feel her pulse rate increasing. She hadn't reacted like this to anyone, she realized, not since Scott.

Oh, there'd been a number of flirtations, but that was all they ever amounted to, just casual flirtations. Not a single one of those flirtations ever went beyond that initial, shallow stage. Not because the other party hadn't been willing, but because she hadn't.

In all this time, she had been neither willing nor ready to move on. Val remained emotionally immobile because she still loved Scott, but more than that, she didn't want to ever, *ever* hurt again the way she had when she'd learned that Scott was dead. That he wouldn't ever be coming home to her again.

Whoever it was that had said it was better to have loved and lost than never to have loved at all wasn't speaking for her. Because for her, the "lost" part involved a feeling that was akin to having her skin stripped away from her without the benefit of an anesthetic.

It was too painful even to contemplate. She missed being loved, but as far as she was concerned, the pain associated with it was far too great to deal with.

So she heard Rafe's rather personal comment, gave it her own interpretation and while it sped up her heart rate, it still had her keeping steadfast to her flirt-but-don't-follow-through rule.

And this time around, she felt it was better to pretend that she hadn't heard Rafe's slip than to comment on it and perhaps begin something whose ending might just be one that she wasn't able to control or cope with in her usual fashion.

As if to cover up his words in case she *had* heard him mumble them under his breath, Rafe asked, "How long do these movies usually take to make?"

That, she thought with relief, was more like it. "Why?" she asked him. "Are you trying to get rid of us already?"

*No, the exact opposite,* he thought. He'd been serious when he'd told her that he couldn't imagine living anywhere else except for Forever, but Val and her crew had brought a measure of excitement to Forever and there was nothing wrong with that. Excitement served as a great contrast to the peace and quiet that usually prevailed in his sleepy little town.

"And chase away all the business that Miss Joan and the rest of the town merchants are seeing? No way. I've got no desire to be lynched. I was just curious," he confessed.

That part was true. He *was* curious, but the added business that store owners were seeing had nothing to do with it. He wanted to know how much time he had left to spend with her. If he knew how many more weeks she would be here—he assumed she was staying for the duration—then he could utilize that time accordingly and make the most of it.

"Well," she began after giving the matter a little thought, "schedules usually depend on the movie being made and the director. Some movies take six months to film, others take half that time and then there are the directors who trust their performers and do one take instead of half a dozen. Jim belongs in that last group, by the way."

Rafe had already been on the set and observed the director in action, so this was nothing new to him. From what he could see, everyone associated with the movie seemed to get along with the tall, unassuming director.

"And just how long does it take for a one-take director to complete shooting a movie?" Rafe asked.

"If there are no unforeseen problems on the set— unexpected weather changes, equipment breaking down, performers coming down with food poisoning or the flu," she elaborated, "it usually takes about six weeks. And that's only because Jim doesn't drive his people." She knew of other directors who demanded nothing short of perfection. They usually got it at the cost of the cast and crew's respect and loyalty. That wasn't Jim's way.

"Which is also why," Val continued, "Jim's got an entire long list of people who've signed up to work for him." She was all but beaming with pride, Rafe noted. Just how close *was* she to this man, he couldn't help wondering. "You won't find a better boss to work for anywhere," she assured him.

"Okay." He laughed. "I'll keep that in mind if I ever

want to work on a movie." Which would be approximately about the time that hell froze over and pigs began to fly, he couldn't help thinking.

"If you ever do decide to do that," Val said, treating his flippant comment seriously, "Give me a call. I'll put you in touch with Jim. Help you find a place to stay," she added.

Their eyes met and held, and for that moment, the surrounding noise emanating from the crowded diner seemed to fade into the background, disappearing along with the people responsible for creating that noise.

For that split second, there was just the two of them and the promise of something more. Something that was left unspoken.

It almost made him consider what she was proposing.

"Something else to keep in mind," he said far more seriously than the comment he'd previously made. Then he'd just been flippant, but he had a feeling there was something more at the heart of her words than there had been earlier.

Rousing himself, Rafe forced his mind to get back on track. The last thing he wanted was to sit there like some tongue-tied idiot, staring at her and coming across like a living brain donor.

"You *are* coming to dinner tonight, right?" he asked her.

His father had invited both her and her mother to dinner at the ranch. The housekeeper had been baking and preparing things since yesterday.

He was rewarded with a smile that was at least one-thousand-watts bright. "Wouldn't miss it for the world," she told him.

"And your mother—" While his father had denied that the whole point of having this dinner was in order to have Val's former-actress mother over, Rafe knew for a fact that it was. His father, he'd observed, was all but singing. The man hadn't appeared this lighthearted since before their mother had taken ill and died.

"—is coming, too," Val assured him, completing his sentence for him.

"Good." He didn't want to have to deal with the disappointed version of his father should the former actress not be coming over. "My dad hasn't stopped talking about having your mother over for dinner since he extended the invitation to you a couple of days ago. It's like looking into the past and seeing what he had to have been like, anticipating going on his very first date," Rafe told her.

A second later, he realized what he'd just said and how that had to have sounded to her. "Not that this is a date. He doesn't think of it that way," he denied. "After all, your mother's married and I wouldn't want you to think that my dad, that he—" Any second now, his tongue was literally going to tie itself into a knot, he thought, not seeing a way out of this verbal maze he'd trapped himself into.

Val came to his rescue, feeling that he had really suffered enough. "What I think—what my mother thinks," she added to further ease his mind, "is that she's having dinner with an extremely loyal fan of her earlier acting career. I can tell you that she's really looking forward to it. It's been a while since someone saw her as the actress she once was instead of the casting director that she's become.

"Don't get me wrong, my mother loves her work, loves the business, but I think that at times, she misses being in front of the cameras, misses having the camera capture her best side, things like that. She is more than happy to have dinner with your dad and the rest of your family."

He nodded, taking it all in. "Good, because he's really talked about nothing else for days. He's making Mike and Ray clean the place up as if the queen of England was coming. Even the stables smell fresh," he told her with a wide grin. "I know that he would have roped Alma in, too, to help, except that Alma's busy working." *And being pregnant,* he couldn't help thinking. He wondered just when his sister was going to tell the family the news. To his recollection, his sister had never been the superstitious kind, afraid of saying something in case that jinxed it. But then, having a kid did change everything, according to Eli.

"Did your father try to 'rope you in,' too?" Val asked.

She tried to picture Rafe with his sleeves rolled up, on his hands and knees, washing the floor or something equally as out of character. The image wouldn't take. The Rafes of the world were overseers, straw bosses, not worker bees. At least, not *those* kind of worker bees, she amended.

"Actually, no," he told her. "Dad thought that you— or Jim—might need me for something connected to the movie." He looked a little uncomfortable as he told her,

"You know, I really feel like I'm taking unfair advantage of your boss," he confessed.

"Why would you feel that?" she asked. She hadn't known the man all that long and granted she was going basically by a gut feeling, but she couldn't see Rafe being the type to take advantage of anyone. The man was just too honest.

"Well, Jim's paying me to be a consultant," he reminded her. "I thought maybe he was kidding, but I keep getting handed these checks."

She was still waiting for him to get to the negative part. "And the problem is…?"

"Well, I haven't really been 'consulted' about anything," he told her. "So I'm getting money under false pretenses."

She knew of so many people who would have not only taken the money in this situation, but argued for some sort of a raise.

With a laugh, she brushed her lips against his cheek, intending it to be a harmless sign of affection—telling herself that it was nothing more significant than that. Also, telling herself that she had to be less unguarded about these meaningless demonstrations of affection.

"God, but you are one of a kind, Rafe Rodriguez. Let's just say that Jim likes covering all his bases and this way he knows that if he *does* need to find out something about the locals, or where he could find, let's say the most romantic place to film a scene, he's got someone to turn to. It helps keep him focused," she told Rafe.

He was still a little uncertain about all this. "So this isn't taking advantage?"

She put it another way for him. "If giving someone peace of mind is taking advantage, then yes, you're taking advantage of him."

She looked at him for a long moment. After being around people who told half-truths and came up with creative fiction that had nothing to do with scripts and storyboards, but were meant only to take advantage of a situation, Rafe was like a fresh spring breeze.

A very sexy fresh spring breeze.

"Why are you looking at me like that?" he asked her, unable to understand her expression.

He found her smile almost shy as she said, "Because I thought that men like you had something in common with unicorns," she told him. He raised a quizzical eyebrow and she explained, "You both didn't exist."

"Well, I don't know about a unicorn, but I exist." Rafe put his hand over hers. "Maybe tonight, after dinner, I can find a way to prove it to you."

There was that warm shiver again, she thought, dancing up and down her spine. Making her anticipate things she had no business anticipating because she wasn't going to allow it to go anywhere.

Rather than laugh or say something dry or witty, she heard someone with her voice answer him by saying, "Maybe."

*Oh, God,* she groaned inwardly. She was turning out to be her own worst enemy.

"YOU HAVE A lovely, lovely home here, Mr. Rodriguez," Gloria Halladay enthused as she sat back in her chair and looked around the dining room with its massive long dark table and ten imposing chairs. Despite that, there was a cozy feel to the evening since dinner turned out to be just the four of them.

"Call me Miguel, please," Rafe's father requested. Tonight, after careful, painstaking grooming, Miguel looked more like a landowner from eras gone by. "And if my home is lovely, it is because you are gracing it with your presence. Yours and your daughter's," he amended, nodding toward Val.

The compliment had been structured to include both the women, but Miguel's eyes were all but exclusively riveted on the former actress.

Gloria sighed at the compliment. "Valentine, I have *got* to have your father come out here and take lessons from this man." She looked at her host with warmth. "You make all those lovely things sound true."

"Oh, but they are," he assured her. "You are every bit as beautiful as you were the first time I saw you on the screen. The movie was *My Favorite Fiancée,*" he recalled.

"I knew there was a reason why our vision goes as we get older," Gloria responded with a good-natured laugh.

The laugh faded into a sincere smile. "You flatter me, Miguel."

"Flattery has nothing to do with it," he protested with alacrity. "I taught all my children to speak the truth. What kind of a father would I be if I didn't set an example and follow my own teaching?"

"A very diplomatic one," Gloria countered with a wink.

"Diplomacy has nothing to do with it, either," Miguel answered. Without realizing it, he began to rub his chest with small, concentric circles. Something he'd eaten was beginning to weigh rather heavily on him. Indigestion began to burn a small path up his throat and down through his chest. "But I can see that I am embarrassing you so I will change the subject and admire you in the silence of my heart."

He shifted in his chair, suddenly feeling uncomfortable and unable to remedy the problem. Trying to focus on something else, Miguel looked down at his guest of honor's plate. "I see you have done justice to Juanita's lamb. My housekeeper will be well pleased. Would you care for some more?" he asked.

Miguel was already on his feet, ready to fetch more since the serving dish on the table was empty. Perspiration popped up along his brow but he did his best to ignore it. When had the room gotten so unseasonably hot?

"I can get—"

"No, please, I'm full," Gloria protested, clearly not wanting her host to put himself out.

At that point, Miguel dropped back into his chair, but his special guest's protest had nothing to do with it. He could feel his face turning clammy—was it pale? How could it be when the pain he felt radiating from his chest was so red hot?

*It will pass. This will pass. Just like the other pains I have had before have passed,* Miguel told himself, silently repeating the words like a mantra, willing the wave back at the same time that he lamented its onset at this of all times.

For a moment, everything around him mysteriously moved into the distance, receding as a strange darkness encroached on him. It reduced the very light around him to almost a pinprick—just as the pain was sharpest.

He might have given in completely, had he not heard the voice calling to him.

Calling him back.

In his present state, as perspiration continued to form along his forehead, seeping into his eyes, he didn't realize that it was Rafe's voice calling to him.

Didn't even realize that he had somehow managed to bonelessly slide from his chair onto the floor where he now lay.

"Dad! Dad, can you hear me?"

Rafe was right beside him, trying to rouse his father, fearing the worst. Out of the corner of his eye, he saw Val take out her phone.

It wouldn't do any good, he thought in despair. Everyone was too far away. The nearest hospital was fifty miles from here.

"There's nobody to call, we don't have 9-1-1 for medical emergencies. Call—"

Rafe was about to rattle off the phone number of the town's only doctor when he stopped short.

For thirty years, Forever had existed without any kind of a physician in its town and then one day, three years ago, Daniel Davenport showed up in their midst to open up a practice. He'd been working practically nonstop since he'd arrived. Deciding to take a much overdue vacation, he had just recently taken his wife—the sheriff's sister-in-law—and their children back to New York, his birthplace.

That left Forever without any sort of medical help. And his father, Rafe thought, feeling desperate, without hope.

"I'm not calling 9-1-1," she told him. "I'm calling—" A voice came on the line and she stopped talking to Rafe and addressed the person she'd called. "Doc, it's Val. Listen, Miguel Rodriguez, the man whose ranch we're using in the film, just grabbed his chest and crumbled to the floor. Yes," she said, answering his question, "I think it's a heart attack. How fast can you get here?" she asked. "Grab the sheriff. He can get you up here by the fastest route. And Doc—*hurry,*" she added but she was already talking to a dial tone. The set doctor had hung up on her and was on his way.

Turning to reassure Rafe and tell him that the production crew's doctor was on his way, she saw that her mother was kneeling over Miguel, giving the unconscious man CPR.

The situation was deadly serious, as serious as it'd been a minute ago, but the ironic humor in it still didn't escape her. Her mother was old school and was administering CPR the original way, counting out measured compressions on Miguel's chest and alternating that with mouth-to-mouth resuscitation.

Val moved over to stand next to Rafe. "Your dad's going to regret not being conscious for that," she commented.

*As long as he lives,* Rafe thought uneasily. "You got

a doctor on the phone?" he asked her. When Val nodded, he asked, mystified, "How?"

Lucky thing they had come to film here, she couldn't help thinking. "Every movie has its own set doctor. We can't get insured without one."

Rather than enlighten him, her answer just puzzled him. "Insured?"

Val nodded. "Movies have to be insured just like businesses, except our insurance is to cover against unforeseeable delays. One of which is having someone become suddenly ill. In a couple of extreme cases, the main star died and there was a scramble to replace them. Schedules were delayed, crews still had to be paid—insurance covers all that." She flashed him a compassionate smile. "More information than you wanted to know, right?"

"No, this is good," Rafe answered, clearly preoccupied by what was going on a couple of feet away from him.

He heard his father moan. To him, it was a beautiful sound. It meant that the man was breathing again. Rafe closed his eyes, offering up a quick prayer.

Val's mother sat back on her heels for a moment, carefully watching his father's face, an expression of satisfaction gracing her features. "I think he's going to be okay," she told Rafe without turning around to face him.

"Lucky thing you two came to dinner," Rafe said, an incredible wave of relief washing over him.

"Lucky thing," Val echoed.

She didn't realize that she'd wrapped her fingers around his and was squeezing his hand now.

But he did.

It gave him strength and, oddly enough, hope.

## Chapter Fifteen

As was typical on one of Jim Sinclair's movies, shooting was going very well and was well ahead of schedule. Since so much of the film was now "in the can" and since they *were* in the month of February, to show his appreciation, the romantic comedy director had his assistant, Julian, put together a huge Valentine's Day party for not just the cast and crew but also the citizens of Forever.

Literally *everyone* was welcome.

The food served at the bash represented the combined efforts of the production company's catering service and Miss Joan's two short-order cooks, notably Angel Rodriguez, who was still creating meals in the diner's kitchen that put the town's people in awe—as well as coming back for more.

Sinclair gave the word that no expense was to be spared and he was *always* a man of his word. He wanted this to be a celebration that the town's people would not soon forget.

Surrounded by his family, Miguel Sr. was given a place of honor at the director's table not only because they were using the Rodriguez ranch, both inside and out, in filming the movie but, more importantly, because he was still breathing thanks to the cast's physician and the quick reaction as well as quick thinking on the part of Gloria Halladay.

Grateful though he was to the doctor who had stabilized him, Miguel attributed his being snatched from the very jaws of hell—as he liked to describe it—to the movie star whom he had idolized for a good part of his adult life.

Not for the first time—and still with a deep degree of gratitude—Miguel declared, "Gloria Halladay saved my life," to his son, Eli, who was currently sitting next to him for a moment.

Eli smiled. Like his siblings, he was relieved and grateful to have his father up and moving among them again. For a man who had showed every sign of leaving them for good, Miguel Rodriguez looked amazingly robust and healthy.

"The doctor did help, Dad," Eli pointed out tactfully.

But Miguel shook his head. "No disrespect to the doctor, but Gloria was the one who brought me back from the jaws of hell."

"Is that where you were going, Dad?" Alma asked, suppressing a laugh as she paused to bend over the seated patriarch and brush a quick, affectionate kiss along his cheek. "To hell?"

Miguel snorted, feigning impatience. "You know what I mean, Alma."

"She knows what you mean," Rafe said with certainty, coming up on his father's other side. "By now *everyone* knows what you mean. And the story's getting a little worn-out, Dad," he said with what amounted to a tolerant smile. He supposed, ultimately, he was afraid that his father might embarrass himself. "You do realize that you've been telling it for almost a month now, right?"

"I realize," Miguel replied. "And, the good Lord willing, I will be telling this same story for many months to come. Perhaps even years," he added with a broad smile of anticipation.

"I'm sure you have *lots* of years left to come, Mr. Rodriguez," Val told him as she joined the group growing around Rafe's father.

"This one I like," Miguel said with approval, looking pointedly at Rafe. "She understands my need to share. Is your mother here?" he asked Val. He made no effort to disguise or hide his eager tone.

"My mother loves parties. If she's not here yet, she will be shortly. I've never known her to miss a party she was invited to."

The moment she finished saying that, Val spotted her mother. The latter was standing on the far side of the huge circuslike tent that had been erected to accommodate the large number of people attending. Beckoning her over, Val waved her hand above her head until her mother saw her. The latter disengaged herself from the people she was talking to and began to make her way over through the thickest part of the crowd.

When she joined them, Gloria's attention immediately focused on the man she realized was sitting at the center of this group. "How are you feeling, Miguel?" she asked warmly.

"Like a new man," he told her. "Like a very blessed new man, thanks to you."

"Well, I'm just very happy that I was there to help," she replied. The conversation swiftly changed from a group discussion to a dialogue between the two older people, both veterans in their worlds.

"Thank your mother for humoring my dad," Rafe said to her as they walked away from the table. He glanced over his shoulder and saw that his brothers and sister had done the same. The movie company wasn't going to be here that much longer and everyone wanted Miguel to live out his fantasy of having Gloria Halladay all to himself for as long as possible.

He, more than anyone, understood that feeling now. Because it was the way he felt about Val. He didn't even want to think about the fact that all this would be over all too soon—and she'd be gone.

"Trust me, Mom's eating this up as much as he is. And she meant what she said. She really is happy she was there for your father. As far as I know, Mom's never saved a life before. This should keep her energized and walking on air for *months,*" Val told him.

She paused to take another sip of the colorful drink in her hand. Alcoholic beverages were at the party courtesy of Jack's. One of the brothers—she'd yet to keep them straight—had given her the first one. The taste had been so satisfying and the drink had gone down so smoothly, she'd tried another.

Val experienced the oddest sensation in her knees and she had to admit that she felt happier than usual.

And even more attracted to Rafe than usual. Or possibly just less inclined to hold fast to the barriers she ordinarily kept in place.

Walking with him now outside the tent, with the star-studded sky above them, looking even more perfect than she thought possible, Val felt very close to Rafe and yet, at the same time, she also felt exceedingly lonely.

Tonight was a night for no secrets.

She missed the touch of a man's hand, missed too the warm, anticipatory tingle while waiting for that all-important kiss, that mind-bending caress.

That contact that made her know she was alive.

She missed what she'd had with Scott.

"You're very quiet tonight," Rafe said, breaking the silence that had been accompanying them on this walk.

Her mouth curved at the sound of his voice, low and velvety, like the sky itself. "Just thinking."

"About?" he asked, coaxing her to say more.

*Say it, Val. You know you want to,* a little voice whispered in her head. *Tell him what's on your mind right now.*

She turned her head just a fraction toward him. "About whether or not you're going to kiss me."

Rafe felt his breath gathering in his chest, turning into a solid entity. A *heavy* solid entity. He stopped walking and faced her. "Which way are you leaning?" he asked her softly.

"If I had a vote," she began, then her voice stopped working for a moment when he slowly caressed her face. "If I had a vote," she repeated a bit more shakily, "it would be yes."

"Good," he murmured, framing her face with his hands. "That's my vote, too," he told her just before his lips covered hers.

Her holidays got crossed and suddenly, it was the Fourth of July with fireworks going off all over inside of her. Flares, magnificent colors, everything that was exciting and new.

For a moment—for a very *long* moment—she allowed herself to sink into the kiss. To revel in it and draw strength from it.

She didn't remember exactly when her arms encircled his neck. There they were, tight around the back of his neck, and she was cleaving to him, her body drawing electricity from his as well as warmth and comfort.

When their lips finally drew apart, she kept her arms where they were, not wanting the bond to be broken just yet.

"Have you ever seen the inside of a movie trailer?" she asked him.

His eyes never left hers as he moved his head from side to side. "Can't say I ever have." God, but she looked particularly delectable tonight, he couldn't help thinking.

"Would you like to?" she whispered.

There were teasing words on the tip of his tongue, flirtatious banter that seemed to come so easily to him whenever he was around her.

But there was something bigger in the way, something that caused him to be serious, because, unlike the other flirtations he'd indulged in, this *was* serious. God help him, but it was.

If he didn't ruin it and back away, afraid of risking a rejection.

Afraid, for the first time, of risking his heart.

He wanted her more than he thought he could possibly want anything or anyone. But he wanted to be sure that this wasn't happening because of those colorful drinks she'd been sipping.

"Val, are you sure about this?"

"Am I sure?" She almost laughed at the irony of the question. "I'm not sure of anything right now, not even name, rank and serial number. But I do know that there's something about you that speaks to me. That makes me want. I haven't wanted for a long time now," she confessed. "Not since…well, not since," she said, leaving the sentence open-ended, unable to make herself say the words that so clearly described Scott's demise. She ran her hands down along the sides of his chest, her eyes still very much on his. "But you, you make me *want*." There was a world of meaning contained in that one unadorned word.

A man could only be so noble, Rafe thought, have so much strength to back off from what came naturally to him, what he wanted so badly. His own supply of strength was swiftly depleting.

Having her here before him, all but telling him she wanted to make love with him when all he could think of—all he'd thought of since he'd first laid eyes on her— was making love with her, the end effect was that it evaporated all his good intentions.

Annihilated his ability to just walk away.

He *couldn't* walk away. Not when his own need for her had just ratcheted up a hundredfold.

"Where did you say this trailer of yours was?" he asked.

Suddenly, she felt almost giddy. This was happening. It was really happening. Oddly enough, consequences didn't enter into it. She, who always thought everything through, didn't want to think about them.

"It's right this way," she answered, tugging on his hand.

"I'll walk you there," he told her, saying the words as if he was just offering to walk her home from the party. In his heart, Rafe knew that was what he *should* do. Walk her to her trailer, see her there safely and then leave.

But when they came to the actual trailer, Rafe just couldn't walk away. For one thing, his fingers were still laced through hers. For another, she was drawing him up the three steps that took him right up to her door— and then through it once she unlocked it.

The moment Val shut the door behind her, the *second* she heard the soft whoosh as the rest of the world outside the trailer was sealed out, the pace, almost languid until now, instantly changed.

Later, Rafe would remember her offering up her mouth to him, would remember pulling her into his arms the instant their lips were sealed. Remember the sensation of being caught up in something that proved to be bigger, more powerful than he was.

Though far from inexperienced, he'd never felt this

before. This was what being caught up in a tornado had to be like.

A thousand sensations hit him at once. Needs, wants, desires and at the top of it all was the driving goal to make this woman happy.

Because her happiness was his.

It was a crazy thought, something he would have attributed as belonging to couples, to married people, neither one of which they were supposed to be, and yet there it was. He wanted to do whatever it took to satisfy her, to make her not regret this once their wild roller-coaster ride came to an end. Because everything ended.

Didn't it?

The second she kissed him, the very moment the door had shut behind her, a door inside of her had sprung open and all the longing she'd thought she had safely secured away from the light of day came flying out, almost stunning her with its strength.

She hadn't been with a man—hadn't *wanted* to be with a man—for so very long. Not since before Scott had died.

But all those emotions hadn't left her, they had merely been biding their time, waiting for the right moment—waiting for the right man—before they showed themselves again.

And now that they had, she couldn't restrain them, couldn't make them subside or go away. They were almost burning her up from the inside out.

Desperate to touch him and to be touched *by* him, Val tugged at his clothing, stripping him bare as quickly and as eagerly as he was stripping her.

Her body was on fire even before it entwined with Rafe's. And though she could see that he wanted her, he didn't immediately take what at this moment was clearly his.

He surprised her by taking his time, by passing his hands along her body, arousing her to heights she hadn't known were possible. Increasing the magnitude and depth of what she was feeling to such degrees it made her almost believe that she had to be delirious, that something this good, this exquisite just couldn't be happening.

And yet, it was.

Rafe set every inch of her on fire with his lips, with his surprisingly gentle touch until she all but threw him down beneath her on her bed and then quickly straddled him.

"If you don't take me now—" she began hoarsely and then had no strength to finish the line, no "threat" prepared to levy against him if he didn't show her some mercy and complete the act of lovemaking with her right here, right now.

It didn't matter.

He understood.

Suddenly, their positions were reversed again and she was the one beneath him.

His eyes met hers and she could feel her very breath siphoning away from her. Time seemed to literally stand still, then go into slow motion.

His fingers caressed her, priming her before he moved her legs farther apart. Before he entered her and became one with her.

Just as she wanted.

As she caught her breath again, he began to move, at first slowly, then increasing his tempo in mind-bending increments.

Val mimicked his movements, doing what she could to catch up. When she did, they moved as one, going faster and faster, their bodies as sealed together as their lips.

A cry of ecstasy bubbled up within her until it finally exploded just as the rest of her world did, raining down on her in a host of colorful lights and sensations and, oh, such wonderful feelings.

She clung to him, her fingertips going deeply into his forearms.

Val didn't realize that her nails were digging into his flesh. All she knew was that she had to hold on for dear life. Hold on for as long as she could because if she loosened her grip, the sensation would leave. And she desperately didn't want it to.

Because for the first time in a very long time, she felt safe.

She felt as if she was home.

## Chapter Sixteen

The next moment, the very same feelings Val just experienced had the exact opposite effect on her.

Rather than making her feel safe, she was terrified. Terrified because her feelings were so strong and she knew in her heart that if she allowed them to overtake her, allowed them to take root, she was literally setting herself up for the very same hurt that all but tore her apart when she discovered that Scott had been killed.

At that time, the emptiness that had engulfed her had been so huge, so bottomless, she didn't think she would ever stop free-falling through space. Though she hadn't let anyone know, for a long while it had been touch and go whether or not she'd be able to pull herself together and go on with her life.

And what she'd felt here, tonight, for Rafe after making love with him had the very same dimensions to it. Falling in love again was out of the question. She refused to do it, absolutely refused, she thought fiercely. Because, this time, if something happened to him, to Rafe, she wouldn't survive. Not twice when she'd barely made it once.

It was far better not to put herself in that kind of jeopardy.

She let out a long breath, as if to purge her feelings from her soul, to expel them as if they'd never been there, never existed.

Her body shuddered with the effort.

So THIS WAS what it was like, what Eli, Gabe and Alma were so sold on. This was what it felt like to be in love, Rafe thought as the world around him slowly came back into focus. For him, the exact sensation defied description. He began to understand why Eli had spent so long pining after Kasey, loving her even after she'd married another man, being there for her no matter what. Patiently hoping even when there appeared to be no hope. Until there was.

He felt like bursting with glee, felt like running onto the rooftop and shouting out to the world to let it know that he was in love with his own personal Valentine.

Skimming his lips along the side of Val's neck, he wanted to make love with her again, but this time far more slowly than the first. This time—

Rafe felt the difference in her instantly. One moment Val had been soft, supple, her body curving into his and although they had just made love, he could feel himself responding to her again. Wanting her all over again. The next moment, he could feel her stiffening, drawing back, as if she was pulling herself back into some invisible shell.

Gathering herself together and away from him.

What had changed?

"Val? What's wrong?" he asked after she made no attempt to respond to the unspoken question in his voice when he said her name.

"I shouldn't have done that," she said, her voice so quiet she needed to raise it in order to qualify her words for a whisper.

Had there been some rule he didn't know about, a rule he had unwittingly gone ahead and broken?

Or had regrets suddenly come galloping up to her, regrets that she'd let her guard down, that she'd made love with someone who clearly didn't fit into her world?

"Why?" he pressed in response to her statement. Why was she now telling him that she shouldn't have made love with him? He needed to know.

"Because."

The word remained there, alone and naked and answering nothing. He could feel hurt and anger creeping over him. "You're going to have to give me more than that."

Val's eyes began to sting. "I *gave* you too much as it is."

Was that code? What was that supposed to mean, anyway? "Okay, now you really have me confused."

She pulled the sheet to her as she curled up into a ball, turning her face away from him. "I'm sorry for that, but would you please go?" *Go, before I make you stay, before I ask you to make love with me again and completely destroy the last shred of willpower I have.* "Now," she emphasized. "Please go now."

He couldn't figure out what was going on. His pride bruised, Rafe sat up and grabbed his jeans off the floor. Pulling them on, he stood up, his back to her. "Fine, I'm going. You won't mind if I don't walk out naked." He bit the words off.

She didn't know how long she could hold out, how long she could keep from crying, from grabbing hold of him and asking him to stay.

From begging him to make love with her again and chase away the shadows.

Rafe had a perfect life. He didn't know what it felt like to be afraid of loving someone. Afraid that by loving them, you were setting yourself up for a world of hurt once you lost them. She had no way of making him understand, so she didn't even try.

"Just get dressed and go," she told him hoarsely, dying inside.

Rafe pulled on his boots quickly, punched his arms through the sleeves of his button-down shirt and crossed to the door.

"I'm sorry," was all he said before he left. The words were cold.

The sound of the door being shut hard in his wake echoed through her chest as her tears began to fall. Once set free, they fell faster and faster. She hugged her knees to her chest and buried her head against them.

If she didn't know any better, she would have said that her heart was breaking. But that was impossible since she wasn't in love yet.

And never would be.

FILMING CONTINUED FOR another week and a half. During that time, Val deliberately avoided crossing Rafe's path whenever possible. She assumed he was doing the same with her because he hadn't once sought her out, hadn't come to her and asked to talk.

When avoiding him was impossible, she acted politely, treating him as if he was a stranger. Anyone seeing them could tell that something was definitely wrong between them.

But when Ray, who had worked pretty steadily as one of the background people in the movie, asked him what was going on between the two of them, Rafe all but bit his head off. "There's nothing wrong. You're imagining things."

"I don't have that good an imagination," Ray pointed out.

But Rafe had already walked away.

THE DAYS WENT by, one by one like leaves falling from a tree in autumn. With each day that passed, Rafe knew he was that much closer to never seeing Val again. He spent the next week waging an internal war as to whether or not to come see her one last time, to ask her what happened, to wish her well or just to look at her before she permanently slipped out of his life, a mirage he obviously couldn't possess.

The internal war had its ups and downs. The upshot was that it left him utterly inert—and not just a little surly.

He took on projects—nothing was too small or too large—and worked from one end of the day to the other.

It didn't help. His disposition, the rest of his family noted, continued to grow surlier.

As the last day of filming approached, his family was having a harder and harder time dealing with this new version of Rafe that constantly muttered under his breath as he went storming his way through daily life.

Finally, urged on by his father, Mike confronted Rafe on the range as the latter worked to fix another length of fence that had gone down. Mike drove up, parked his Jeep beside Rafe's and got out. Rafe, he noted, didn't even bother looking his way.

"What's going on with you?" Mike demanded without any preamble as he walked up to him. "You've been out of sync ever since the night of the Valentine party. What happened? She turn down your best moves?" Mike laughed, trying to kid Rafe out of his surly shell.

And then he stopped, scrutinizing Rafe's expression. "She *didn't* turn you down, did she?" Rafe still made no answer, but he didn't have to. Mike could see the answer in his brother's eyes. "So, what's the problem? You find that you're falling for her and you're afraid if she finds out, she'll clip your wings?"

There was no way Rafe was about to go into any details. The whole experience was far too painful for him to share, so he went with what had originally troubled him before everything had blown up in his face. "The problem is that she's going to be leaving."

"So? Ask her to stay," Mike suggested.

Rafe looked at him as if he'd lost his mind. "For what?" he demanded.

"For you, I thought."

"Right," Rafe sneered, swinging his hammer against the post and driving a nail in so hard, the barbed wire shimmied. "She's part of a glamorous business, her mother's an actress—"

"Ex-actress," Mike interjected mildly.

Rafe gave him a dirty look, as if that point was too minor to even bother correcting. "Okay. But her parents are successful. What have *I* got to offer her?"

Mike leaned against the post that had been reinforced earlier, folding his arms across his chest. "Well, you're not exactly a pauper, you know. You've got a share in a pretty successful ranch."

Which amounted to a nice sum, Rafe granted, but "nice" wasn't what was needed here—even *if* that was the only obstacle in the way. "I repeat, what have I got to offer her?"

Mike watched at him for a long moment, as if assessing what he felt he saw in his brother's expression, in his body language.

"What about love? Unless, of course," Mike allowed with a shrug, "you don't love her."

Denial sprang to Rafe's lips—but what was the point? Loving Val didn't change anything, at least not for her. "Yeah, I do." Even though he'd wanted to issue a denial, all that had come out of his mouth was an affirmative answer. Even his head was turning against him. Forget about his heart, Rafe thought disgruntled.

"So go for it," Mike urged. "Ask her to stay. What's the worse that can happen? She'll leave? Well, that's what's happening now and this way, at least you have a shot at keeping her here. Look, Rafe, you've got nothing to lose by asking her and everything—according to what I see—to lose if you don't."

Dropping the hammer to the ground, Rafe ran the back of his arm against his forehead, wiping away his sweat. "Will you shut up and stop nagging me if I go?"

"No," Mike admitted truthfully, then added, "but it's a start."

Muttering a few new choice things under his breath, Rafe picked up his shirt off the post where he'd hung it and pulled it back on. "Take over," was all he said as he moved to climb into his Jeep.

"I always do," Mike called out after him, then added, "Good luck!"

Rafe waved his hand over his head in acknowledgement but didn't look back.

He wasn't going to ask her to stay—what was the point? Rafe thought—but he *was* going to ask her what happened, why when everything seemed to be going so well between them it had suddenly blown up. She owed him some sort of an explanation.

She owed him at least that much.

THE SET WHERE some of the filming had taken place looked like a ghost town in miniature, or at least what he suspected one would look like once the lifeblood had been drained out of a town.

Accustomed now for the past seven weeks to seeing people hustling about with special hand cameras focused on small sections of the set at a time, now there was no camera or any sort of action to focus on. In addition, true to Val's promise, everything had been cleaned up. There was no trash, no debris lying around or floating on the wind.

But along with the trash, the sounds of life were gone, as well. It only went to underscore the emptiness he was feeling. In his gut he knew that getting over Val would be rough, maybe even impossible, at least at first.

Who was he kidding? It was going to take a long, long time.

It hadn't hit him just how hard it was going to hurt—and just how much he didn't want her to go—until this very moment, as he stood looking around the empty set. Leaving his Jeep where it was, he broke into a run, heading to the site where her trailer had been parked, praying that it was still there, that she hadn't already taken off.

His heart was in his throat by the time he reached his destination.

The trailer was still there.

His adrenaline spiked. Rafe doubled his speed as he ran up the steps to the front door.

"Val," he called, pounding on the door. "Are you in there? Val, open up, I have to talk to you!"

"Now?"

The voice asking the question came from behind him. Swinging around, he saw Val standing there, looking at him in apparent confusion.

"We're packing up to leave by nightfall," she told him coolly, proud of herself for holding it together. Wondering how long she could manage to continue doing that. "If you wanted to talk, you should have come earlier."

He came down the steps, fighting the urge just to

pull her into his arms. To kiss her senseless and defy her to tell him that she wasn't feeling *something*. But for now, he held himself in check, hoping to appeal to her reason. "I'm here now."

She deliberately avoided looking into his face as she began to push past him to get to the trailer. "I don't have time to—"

He caught her by the arm as she tried to pass him. "Make time."

It wasn't an order, it was an entreaty.

She raised her chin defiantly. "Why should I? You all but went into hiding for the past ten days."

He stared at her incredulously. Was she serious? Why was she turning this around, making it *his* fault? She was the one who'd started it. "You threw me out of your trailer, remember?"

Her eyes narrowed. "You didn't even try to come back. If I had meant anything at all to you, you would have tried to work things out instead of accepting the situation and just walking away."

Damn, there really should be some kind of a self-help book when it came to understanding women. "I thought you didn't want to see me," he emphasized.

She'd given him more credit than that. He had to know what she was doing, what she was *hoping* he would do in turn. She'd needed to have all her fears allayed and he'd just gone silent on her, accepting what she said at face value and going away—as if she didn't mean anything to him.

"And you weren't even curious why?" she demanded now.

All he'd known at the time was she wanted nothing to do with him—and it really, really hurt. "It was enough that you didn't want me around."

She shook her head. This was pointless. She was better off just concentrating on healing and forgetting about nebulous happily-ever-after endings that never materialized. "Look, I've got to—"

Rafe moved quickly, blocking her way to the trailer. Feeling like a man who was about to go down for the third time, he tried another approach. "Is there any chance that you might want to someday stay in a town like this? Not now," he underscored so she wouldn't feel as if he was rushing her, "but someday?"

Hadn't he been paying attention these past seven weeks? "In case you haven't noticed, I *have* been staying in a town like this."

She'd only been here as part of her work. He wasn't talking about that. "No, I mean for longer."

About to dismiss the topic, Val saw something in his eyes, something that spoke to her, saying things that he hadn't put into actual words yet. She decided to let whatever was going on here play itself out. "How long is 'longer' and exactly why would I be staying?"

He struggled for a moment, his protective side warring with the side that desperately wanted her to stay, or to at least come back. In the end, that side won out and he was honest with her.

"Because I can't make it knowing that when you leave, you won't be back. I have to believe that you'd be coming home to me no matter how long it took."

Was he actually saying what she thought he was saying? "Rafe—"

He held his hand up to stop her. "Let me finish," he requested. "If I stop, I'll never be able to say this. And I need to say it. Look, I get it. You need to be in the family business and this is a little hick town to you, but that night, after the party, I felt like there was something special going on between us. We weren't just two people having really, really great sex. I felt a real connection with you, felt something strong taking hold and maybe that's scary for you but I don't think we should just throw it away because one of us is scared. This kind of thing doesn't happen very often. It's like that comet thing—" He searched for a name.

"Haley's Comet?" Val supplied.

"That's the one. It doesn't come through very often. Neither does what we have between us. If we don't hitch a ride on it now, we might never hitch a ride at all."

Val blinked, trying to process what he was saying— and what he meant by it. "Are you proposing to me?"

Momentarily stunned, he shrugged helplessly. "Kinda. Sort of." Oh, hell, he might as well call a spade a spade. "Yes, yes I am," he finally told her, laying himself bare. He watched her eyes as he asked, "What do you say?"

"What I say is that that has to be the strangest proposal on record." And one that she felt he probably regretted making, even now. "Look, Rafe, it's not that I don't have feelings for you—"

"Just 'feelings'?" he questioned. If she really didn't love him, he needed to know now, before he made an even bigger fool of himself than he already had.

And then she said something that he was unprepared for, something that blew him right out of the water. "All right, I love you," she cried. "But that's just the problem. I've been married once and losing Scott almost killed me. I don't want to have to go through that again." She saw him opening his mouth to speak and she cut him off with one final argument. "And you can't promise me that you won't die."

"No, I can't," he agreed quietly. "But I can promise to love you with my last ounce of strength until I do."

She could feel the tears gathering up, but this time, they were tears of joy. He'd genuinely moved her. "Oh, damn you, Rafe, why'd you have to go and say that?"

"Because I mean it," he told her, slipping his arms around her. "I love you. Whether you stay or go, that's not going to change how I feel about you. We're a very steadfast bunch, the people in my family. And when we fall in love, it's forever. That part's not going to change, whether you go or stay, but I'd really rather that you stay—or at least come home to me after each film is rolled."

"Wrapped," she corrected, biting back a laugh. Val sighed. "I guess I have to stick around. Someone's got to teach you the proper terms of my industry. It might as well be me."

"And the proposal?" he asked. "What's your verdict on that?"

She threaded her arms around his neck. "I guess that's a yes, too."

"Good answer."

He kissed her then, before she could say something else or come up with another stumbling block to put in his path. He kissed her for a long time—just to be sure.

\* \* \* \* \*

*Don't miss Marie Ferrarella's next romance,*
*MISSION: CAVANAUGH BABY,*
*available September 2013*
*from Harlequin Romantic Suspense!*

# REQUEST YOUR FREE BOOKS!
## 2 FREE NOVELS PLUS 2 FREE GIFTS!

**⊞ HARLEQUIN®**

*American ★ Romance®*

### LOVE, HOME & HAPPINESS

**YES!** Please send me 2 FREE Harlequin® American Romance® novels and my 2 FREE gifts (gifts are worth about $10). After receiving them, if I don't wish to receive any more books, I can return the shipping statement marked "cancel." If I don't cancel, I will receive 4 brand-new novels every month and be billed just $4.74 per book in the U.S. or $5.24 per book in Canada. That's a savings of at least 14% off the cover price! It's quite a bargain! Shipping and handling is just 50¢ per book in the U.S. and 75¢ per book in Canada.* I understand that accepting the 2 free books and gifts places me under no obligation to buy anything. I can always return a shipment and cancel at any time. Even if I never buy another book, the two free books and gifts are mine to keep forever.

154/354 HDN F4YN

| | |
|---|---|
| Name | (PLEASE PRINT) |

| | |
|---|---|
| Address | Apt. # |

| | | |
|---|---|---|
| City | State/Prov. | Zip/Postal Code |

Signature (if under 18, a parent or guardian must sign)

**Mail to the Harlequin® Reader Service:**
**IN U.S.A.:** P.O. Box 1867, Buffalo, NY 14240-1867
**IN CANADA:** P.O. Box 609, Fort Erie, Ontario L2A 5X3

**Want to try two free books from another line?**
**Call 1-800-873-8635 or visit www.ReaderService.com.**

* Terms and prices subject to change without notice. Prices do not include applicable taxes. Sales tax applicable in N.Y. Canadian residents will be charged applicable taxes. Offer not valid in Quebec. This offer is limited to one order per household. Not valid for current subscribers to Harlequin American Romance books. All orders subject to credit approval. Credit or debit balances in a customer's account(s) may be offset by any other outstanding balance owed by or to the customer. Please allow 4 to 6 weeks for delivery. Offer available while quantities last.

**Your Privacy**—The Harlequin® Reader Service is committed to protecting your privacy. Our Privacy Policy is available online at www.ReaderService.com or upon request from the Harlequin Reader Service.

We make a portion of our mailing list available to reputable third parties that offer products we believe may interest you. If you prefer that we not exchange your name with third parties, or if you wish to clarify or modify your communication preferences, please visit us at www.ReaderService.com/consumerschoice or write to us at Harlequin Reader Service Preference Service, P.O. Box 9062, Buffalo, NY 14269. Include your complete name and address.

HAR13R

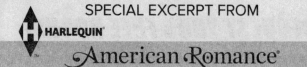
*Check out this excerpt from*
*CALLAHAN COWBOY TRIPLETS*
*by Tina Leonard,*
*coming September 2013.*

*Tighe, the wildest of the Callahan brothers, is determined*
*to have his eight seconds of glory in the bull-riding ring—*
*but gorgeous River Martin throws off his game!*

Tighe Callahan sized up the enormous spotted bull. "Hello,
Firefreak," he said. "You may have bested my twin, Dante,
but I aim to ride you until you're soft as glove leather. Gonna
retire you to the kiddie rides."

The legendary rank bull snorted a heavy breath his way,
daring him.

"You're crazy, Tighe," his brother Jace said. "I'm telling
you, that one wants to kill you."

"Feeling's mutual." Tighe grinned and knocked on the
wall of the pen that held the bull. "If Dante stayed on him
for five seconds, I ought to at least go ten."

Jace looked at Tighe doubtfully. "Sure. You can do it.
Whatever." He glanced around. "I think I'll go get some
popcorn and find a pretty girl to share it with. You and Firefreak just go ahead and chat about life. May be a one-sided
conversation, but those are your favorite, anyway."

Jace wandered off. Tighe studied the bull, who never
broke eye contact with him, his gaze wise with the scores
of cowboys whom he'd mercilessly tossed, earning himself

a legendary status.

"Hi, Tighe," River Martin said, and Tighe felt his heart start to palpitate. Here was his dream, his unattainable brunette princess—smiling at him as sweet as cherry wine. "We heard you're going to ride a bull tomorrow, so the girls and I decided to come out and watch."

This wasn't good. A man didn't need his concentration wrecked by a gorgeous female—nor did he want said gorgeous, unattainable female to see him get squashed by a few tons of angry luggage with horns.

But River was smiling at him with her teasing eyes, so all Tighe could say was, "Nice of you ladies to come out."

River said, "Good luck," and Tighe shivered, because he did believe in magic and luck and everything spiritual. And any superstitious man knew it was taunting the devil himself to wish a man good luck when the challenge he faced in the ring was nothing compared to the real challenge: forcing himself to look into a woman's sexy gaze and not drown.

He was drowning, and he had been for oh, so long.

*Look for CALLAHAN COWBOY TRIPLETS*
*by Tina Leonard, coming September 2013, only from*
*Harlequin® American Romance®.*

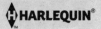
**HARLEQUIN**®

# American Romance®

## Wounded in love and war.

Ex-marine Buck Summerhayes wants to put the past
behind him. He finds peace working at the Teton Valley
Dude Ranch, a special place for families of fallen soldiers.
Maybe one day, he'll have a family of his own—right
now, he can't afford to indulge in dreams.

Alexis Wilson is no dream. Tasked with overseeing Alex
and her young ward during their visit to the ranch, Buck
finds himself falling for both the woman and the little
girl. Like Buck, Alex has had more than her share of
heartache. But maybe between them, they can build a
future that's still full of possibilities.

## *Home to Wyoming*

# by REBECCA WINTERS

**Dare to dream on September 3, only from
Harlequin® American Romance®.**